SWANSEA SPY

SWANSEA SPY

Geraint Thomas

First published in 2011

ISBN: 978-1-84524-183-4

Cover illustration: Roger Lewis
Cover design: Gwasg Carreg Gwalch

Published by Llygad Gwalch,
12 Iard yr Orsaf, Llanrwst, Wales LL26 0EH
tel: 01492 642031
fax: 01492 641502
email: books@carreg-gwalch.com
internet: www.carreg-gwalch.com

For my parents,
who enabled me to dream,
and Gruffydd and Ioan,
who have only just begun.

Contents

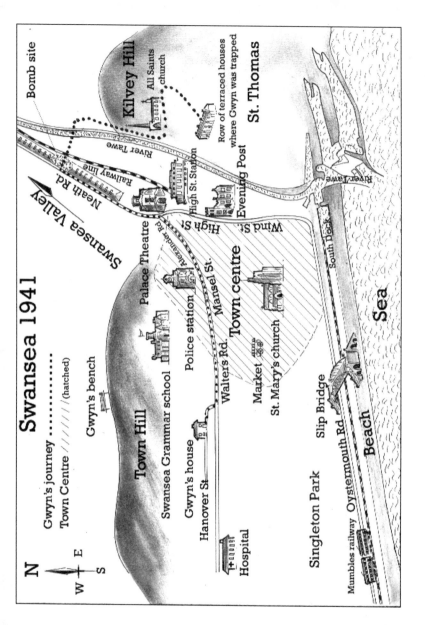

Swansea 1941

Prelude

In the early hours of 27 June 1940, a solitary German plane flew over Swansea and dropped ten bombs on the unsuspecting town below. Luckily nobody was hurt. Over the next few years there were to be another forty-three attacks, lasting a combined total of seventy-two hours, involving 1,273 high-explosive bombs and 56,000 incendiary devices. These destroyed 857 properties, damaged a further 11,000, killed 230 people and injured a further 409.

Swansea Spy is a fictional story set against this true backdrop. As far as the author understands, all the references to the town and the war years are factually correct, although, in the interests of developing the narrative, some liberties have been taken over the timing of the first attack and what became known as the 'Three Nights' Blitz', from 19 to 21 February 1941, when the bombs fell for a total of thirteen hours.

As for the main protagonist's surname, Lazenby, it is a salute to the late Ralph Lazenby, a gentle old Swansea soldier who served in the Second World War and was one of the founding members of the SAS.

Chapter 1

Out of the blue
February 1941

It started off as a tiny black dot in the sky, like a bluebottle, but as the three boys splashed in the waves it grew bigger. Soon the drone of its engine made them stop and stare out across the channel.

'What do you reckon it is?' asked 12-year-old Gwyn, as a wave leapt up and soaked the hem of his school shorts.

'It's a Spitfire. Must be going to land at Pembrey airfield,' answered Owen, a tall, wiry boy of the same age, as was the third boy, Tom.

'Na, looks more like a Hurricane to me,' argued Tom. The three friends had decided to stop off on their way home from school and enjoy the first real sunny springlike day of 1941 on the lapping shores of Swansea Bay.

By now the aeroplane was more than halfway over from the north Devon coast and closing in rapidly on the shores of south-west Wales. Gwyn's brown eyes peered intently and his head tilted to one side, as it always did when he was deep in thought.

'I don't know,' overruled Gwyn. 'Its wings look funny to me and it certainly doesn't sound like a Spit.'

The boys stared at the advancing shape in the sky, now the size of a hawk. It started to gain altitude, rising steeply until it disappeared in the midday sun. Then the sound of its engine stopped in an eerie silence that was suddenly broken by a horrific wail as it reappeared, falling out of the sky on to the town below.

'Run – it's a Stuka!' screamed Gwyn.

The boys raced out of the water and tore up the beach. They

scrambled through a gap in the sea defences, but before they could reach the shelter of the sea wall they heard a deafening roar above them and were forced to dive headlong into the sand. The aeroplane screeched over their heads and made straight for the town's South Dock, a few hundred yards away.

Looking up, they could see people scattering for cover on the seafront, which separated the coast from the large basin of water in which several merchant ships were moored. A series of shrill whistles filled the air and three or four loud explosions rattled their brains and made the boys duck their heads to the sand once more. Frightening flashes of flame quickly followed, and huge clouds of smoke started towering above the scene as a shower of debris began to rain down. The boys looked at each other in disbelief.

'They're bombing the docks,' said a stunned Gwyn.

The aeroplane climbed once more into the darkening sky, banked in a steep turn and swooped back over the three friends who, looking up, could just about make out the swastikas beneath its wings. Then the winding wail of an air raid siren began to call out across the town.

'You Nazi cowards,' screamed Owen rising to his feet to wave an angry fist at the aeroplane.

Suddenly a series of sharp cracks were heard and a swarm of small explosions peppered the sky with clouds of grey smoke.

'Get down, Owen,' shrieked Gwyn in panic.

'It's ok, it's the anti-aircraft guns on Ravenhill,' said Tom looking towards the back of the town.

'It's a bit late for that,' said Gwyn sheepishly regaining his composure. 'They're almost out of sight by now.'

He was right. Soon the sound of firing was replaced by the ringing bells of fire engines rushing to the scene.

Owen pulled Gwyn to his feet. 'Come on. Let's go and see what it hit.'

Picking their way carefully in their bare feet, they ran to the steps of the iron Slip Bridge that spanned the coast road and the Mumbles railway line, linking the long beach with the town. After running up two flights of steps the boys caught their breath and looked over towards the docks. Plumes of smoke were dwarfing the huge cranes that had been unloading cargo from the merchant ships that had just arrived from across the Atlantic – one of which was burning.

'Dear God, there's people on fire,' gasped Tom, pointing to several figures blundering about in flames. The three watched in horror as the poor souls threw themselves off the burning deck into the dock, which must have been sixty feet or so below.

The sound of screams carried across the singed air. Gwyn immediately thought of his father somewhere in North Africa with the commandos.

'Is this what it's like for my Dad?' Gwyn asked quietly.

'This is real war all right,' said Owen, solemnly shaking his head.

'They don't tell you about this in the newspaper or on the wireless,' whispered Gwyn to no one in particular.

With the war in its second year, until now all Gwyn had known about it was life on the 'home front' – 'all rations and precautions', his mother had called it – but now it had become real to him. For the first time he was witnessing the chaos and destruction which was raining down over most of Europe; this was his home town in flames, being covered by thick smoke and broken by a very real enemy.

'Come on, let's go and help,' said Tom.

'I'm game,' replied Owen.

But before the boys had time to leave the bridge a loud voice shouted up from the road below.

'What the hell do you think you are doing? Get down from there at once! Do you want to get yourselves killed?'

The boys stared down at an Air Raid Precautions Warden.

'And where are your gas masks?' he demanded with indignation.

'Oh, no,' wailed Gwyn looking towards the incoming tide where three cardboard boxes containing their masks, and three pairs of shoes and socks, were floating in the sea.

As they climbed down the steps another siren rang out across the town, this time signalling the 'all clear'. But the three friends were far from being in the clear as they approached the burly ARP warden, who was waiting to give them a good telling off.

Chapter 2

The Anderson shelter

'Twelve people killed and twenty-six injured, you say. All those poor families. What must they be going through?'

Gwyn's mother was discussing the previous day's air raid with his Uncle Keith at the breakfast table. Gwyn wondered what the two adults would say if they knew just how close he had come to the terrifying event.

'A terrible loss of life,' said Uncle Keith. 'I don't understand why there was no warning. People need to take cover at such times.'

Gwyn looked sheepishly down at his porridge, which was made with water – real milk was rationed, and he hated the taste of dried milk. He stirred in a spoonful of treacle to make it more bearable.

'Talking of which, Gwyn, can you help me in the garden today?' Uncle Keith asked. 'We need to get that shelter finished as soon as possible, before the next raid comes along.'

Usually on a Saturday morning Gwyn would meet his friends and catch the train down to the seaside village of Mumbles to go fishing off the pier, but since the attack Gwyn had struggled to get the sight of flames and the sound of screams out of his head. If truth be told, Gwyn really wanted to stay close to home that day and make sure the family air raid shelter was ready.

'Of course I will,' he said, willing to do anything to make his family safe.

Straight after breakfast Gwyn set about his chores. One of his favourites was feeding Vera and Gracie, their hens. The garden of a Victorian terraced house on Hanover Street was not the most likely place to spot a pair of chickens, but as soon as food rationing

14

had reared its ugly head a year ago, Uncle Keith had returned from a trip to the Gower with the birds in a large basket. Gwyn had wanted to call them Winston and Churchill, until his mother had pointed out that males do not lay eggs, so they settled on their favourite music hall stars, Vera Lynn and Gracie Fields.

'Vera, Gracie! Here, girls', he called, scattering a few handfuls of grain in their run. He then checked the chicken coop, which Uncle Keith had made out of a tea chest with a doorway cut into the wooden side, to find three new eggs – triple the weekly ration!

After completing the rest of his jobs, including cutting sticks and laying the fire in the bedroom ready to be lit in the evening, he joined Uncle Keith back in the garden.

Uncle Keith wasn't his real uncle, he was their lodger, but he had lived with the family for so long that Gwyn and his little sister Molly had come to look upon him as a relative. He worked as a news reporter on the *South Wales Evening Post*. He had tried to join the army and fight at the same time as Gwyn's father had joined up, but he had failed the medical due to an asthmatic chest.

'I'll just have to do my bit by trying to keep people's spirits up on the home front,' he had said when he returned home, looking dejected.

Now he gave Gwyn a friendly smile. 'Well, Gwyn *bach*, let's see if we can't get this done and dusted today.'

They had already prepared a trench around 5 feet deep, but the corrugated metal pieces that formed the main structure of the Anderson shelter were still in a heap in the garden shed. They had to put them together to form an arch, place it in the ground and then cover it with earth.

Between them they made the arch, and Gwyn stood underneath and held it steady while his uncle remained outside and slotted the bolts in place.

'That's it, Gwyn, keep it still.'

Gwyn watched the bolts pop through the holes, helping to guide them where the sections overlapped. When they were all in place his uncle came inside to fix the nuts on and tighten them up.

As they stood admiring their handiwork a voice called out, 'Hey, you in there, time for a break.' They emerged to see Gwyn's mother with two cups of steaming tea in her hands. 'I thought the pair of you could do with the lift. I've even given you each a teaspoon of jam in your tea to keep your strength up.' Gwyn's face lit up – he had really missed sugary things since sugar had been rationed and had become like gold dust.

'Thank you, Mrs Lazenby,' said Uncle Keith taking the cup gratefully. 'We are honoured.'

'If it means having that contraption up and running, instead of lying in a heap, I'd give you all the tea in China.'

'We're not the only ones to be caught out, Mrs Lazenby,' came back Uncle Keith. 'Only half the shelters in Swansea are up as yet.'

'You know me, Mr Jenkins, I don't bother myself with other people's business. I just want what's best for my own family.'

'Well, with this young man's help, it shouldn't take much more than a couple of days,' replied Uncle Keith, winking at Gwyn.

Gwyn smiled over the hot tea cupped in his hands. He felt proud to be able to do something against the war at last, even if it was only making a place to shelter from the destructive power of the Luftwaffe.

With the tea finished, Gwyn's mother gathered up the cups and turned to head back into her kitchen.

'I'd best let you get on,' she said, before looking up at the sky trying to spy an invisible enemy and shaking her head. 'I don't want to be running down to Bethesda's basement in my nightgown if they come again.'

'It shouldn't come to that, Mrs Lazenby. We've broken the back of it now.'

'Good. I'd rather take my chances under the stairs than let the neighbours see me half decent.'

'Well, if you feel like that, why don't you go to bed with your clothes on? That's what some people do.'

'Get out of here, I would feel worse running down the street with my dress all creased!'

Uncle Keith laughed. 'Well, that's your choice – but if I have to write your obituary I'll say, 'She had unrivalled style!" He winked at Gwyn.

'Don't you dare write about me in that paper of yours, dead or alive, or else there will be no more tea for you, Mr Jenkins,' she shrieked in mock anger, before marching back to the house, leaving Gwyn and Uncle Keith chuckling.

By late afternoon the shelter was really taking shape. The structure had been put in place in the ground and the pair had shovelled a large mound of earth from the large garden to cover the roof and sides.

'Are you tired, Gwyn?' asked Uncle Keith resting on his shovel.

'A bit,' the boy answered looking at the blisters beginning to form on his hands.

'Well, let's take a break, and then we need to pop down to the beach.'

'The beach? Whatever for?'

'You'll find out when we get there,' his uncle smiled, pushing away strands of his blonde hair from his piercing blue eyes.

Gwyn smiled back. He loved his 'joking' Uncle Keith, and was glad that he was around while his father was away fighting. He talked with a 'posh' accent, as his father would say, which wasn't south Walian. He was a graduate of Oxford University and seemed to know everything about everything, but he was also very practical and good with his hands.

After a short break Uncle Keith whistled cheerfully past the kitchen door and called for Gwyn. He was pushing a wheelbarrow with a shovel and some sacks inside it. 'Come on, let's get going, it will be teatime before you know it,' he said.

Gwyn followed his uncle down the street. At the corner they passed two workmen busy dismantling the iron railings surrounding a large house. The metal was going to be melted down and used towards making a new tank, battleship or bomber.

In a short time they were on the sandy beach near to where Gwyn and his friends had been playing when the German aeroplane had attacked the docks. The boy felt a sudden pang of guilt now that he stood there with his uncle. Somehow he felt as though he had let him down. Gwyn was relieved when Uncle Keith grabbed a sack and threw it his way, taking him away from his thoughts.

'Right, hold it open while I shovel.'

'Of course, sandbags,' said Gwyn, realising what they were up to.

'Yes, sandbags. We'll need at least thirty of them for the shelter. We're lucky there is so much sand about, there's enough on this beach to mothball Buckingham Palace.'

Gwyn thought about all the sandbags he had seen stacked up outside the main buildings in the town, the police station, the post office, the railway station; they were set up all over Swansea, designed to protect against the results of enemy attacks. Then he thought with a shudder how they had been unable to prevent the carnage at the docks.

After filling six bags and tying them securely they pulled the heavy barrow back home. It was hard going and Uncle Keith had to stop every so often to catch his breath, but the effort would be worth it.

Once home they began packing the sandbags around the shelter and alongside the slope that led down to the entrance. They made three such journeys before dusk began drifting down on to the Welsh seaside town.

'Well, Gwyn,' his uncle said wiping the sweat from his brow, 'I think we had better call it a day, the light has beaten us. I don't know about you but I could do with some of your mother's cawl, even if it is shy of lamb.'

The boy nodded, he was tired and ready for his supper too.

'Have you done your homework yet?'

'Most of it. I've got to learn all the countries in the British Empire.'

'The British Empire.' Uncle Keith smiled wryly. 'There won't be much of that left before long ... if Hitler gets his way.'

'He won't,' said Gwyn firmly.

After packing the tools away the two stood at the entrance to the shelter and watched the sweeping arms of the searchlights roaming across the Swansea sky, picking out the large barrage balloons that were supposed to stop the bombers getting too close to their target. Gwyn thought they looked like pods of silent whales lurking in a sea of darkness.

'Let's hope they don't spot anything tonight. It would be very uncomfortable spending a night in there as it is. We've still got to put the floor down and build some bunk beds to make it a bit more homely. We could be spending a lot of time in there over the coming months.'

'Will this really protect us from the bombs?' asked Gwyn, staring dubiously at their handiwork.

His uncle maintained his gaze on the night sky. 'Well, I know one thing for certain. I would rather be inside a shelter like this than outside when the bombs come. It may not survive a direct hit but it will protect you from all the glass and bricks that get thrown around. That's the worst thing about bombs, the flying debris. At least if one lands on top of you it will all be over in an instant, you won't feel a thing, but I've known people to be in agony for weeks after being caught outside in a blast.'

Gwyn looked at his uncle and nodded seriously to show he understood the gravity of the situation. How did it get like this? The summer before last, he and Dad and Uncle Keith had spent weekends laughing and joking their way through playing football or cricket in the back garden. Now the lawn had been replaced by rows of potatoes and he and Uncle Keith were building an air raid shelter and talking about bombs, and Dad was far away from home in North Africa.

Uncle Keith turned to look Gwyn in the face and said in a serious tone of voice, 'I'm not telling you this to frighten you but to warn you how important it is to take shelter in an air raid, and make sure your mother and sister do so as well. Remember, I may not always be here, and with your father away, you are the man of the house now. Do you understand, Gwyn?'

Gwyn nodded his head. He was the man of the house … the thought filled him with pride and dread at the same time.

'Good. So no more standing on the Slip Bridge during an air raid, do you understand?'

Gwyn blushed. 'How did you find out?'

'I write the news, remember? It's my job to know everything that goes on in this town.'

Chapter 3

Rudely awakened

Gwyn helped his uncle complete the shelter the following Saturday, then his mother added some finishing touches in an attempt to make it more homely. She placed bedding on the bunk beds they had installed and hung a curtain to hide the back wall. Molly thought it great fun and spent hours playing house inside with Rosie, her rag doll. Uncle Keith had told Gwyn's mother to encourage Molly to play in the shelter, saying, 'That way she won't be too scared when we have to use it for real.'

On the Sunday, after they had sat through the morning service at Ebenezer Chapel, Uncle Keith took Gwyn, his mother and Molly for a quiet walk through Singleton Park. Gwyn was surprised to see that large areas of the beautiful grounds had been taken over by a regiment of tired-looking soldiers. It was obvious they had recently returned from some far-off battle or other.

Looking around Gwyn spotted a soldier standing beneath a large tree. He was standing on his own with his back to Gwyn, but there was something familiar about the squareness of his large shoulders and his thick brown hair that made the boy stare.

'Dad?' Gwyn said quietly to himself, not sure of his eyes.

Gwyn began running across the grass towards the man, his heart jumping as wildly as a barrage balloon caught up in a thunder storm.

'Dad!' This time Gwyn called out loud.

The soldier turned around and gave Gwyn a good-natured grin. 'Easy, son, I haven't been here long enough to have children,' he laughed back in a Canadian accent.

'I'm sorry,' answered Gwyn turning red. He felt foolish and

dejectedly turned away. He looked towards his mother and thankfully saw that she had been too busy playing with Molly to notice him making an idiot of himself.

Gwyn joined his uncle, who was chatting to some troops sitting smoking on a bench.

'Looks like you boys have seen some action,' said Uncle Keith, eyeing up their dishevelled appearance. Gwyn knew better than to ask the soldiers why they were in Swansea, but Uncle Keith tried to fish around for information.

'I guess you could say that, sir.' The soldier spoke with the same Canadian accent Gwyn had heard moments earlier.

'Where have you come from?' asked Uncle Keith.

'Now you don't expect to get an answer to that, do you?'

'You can't blame a journalist for trying,' laughed Uncle Keith, 'Anyway, you boys enjoy your stay in Swansea. You deserve it, by the looks of you.'

Gwyn found it difficult getting off to sleep that night. Thinking he had seen his father in the park had upset him and thoughts of the war tumbled around inside his head.

Sitting up, he relit the candle on the nightstand next to his bed and reached for a photograph of his father. It had been taken just before he had left for duty. He was in his uniform and smiling brightly at the camera. The photograph brought a massive pang of longing to his heart. He buried his face into his father's large winter overcoat, which lay on top of his bedclothes for extra warmth. It smelt of his father's favourite tobacco, and tears began to moisten his eyes. 'I mustn't cry,' he scolded himself.

Eventually Gwyn decided to fetch himself a glass of water. He climbed out of bed, taking the candle with him to guide his way. Making his way across the landing he stopped outside his mother's bedroom and looked through the open door. Molly was

22

sleeping peacefully next to her mother; Gwyn had to fight the urge to join the comforting warmth.

On the stairs Gwyn stopped in his tracks – there were noises coming from downstairs. It was nearly midnight, his mother and sister were fast asleep, and Uncle Keith was on the night shift at work. Gwyn heard his uncle's voice in his head saying, 'you're the man of the house'. Blowing the candle out and placing it on a step Gwyn crept on cautiously, stopping by the umbrella stand in the hall to pick up a heavy walking stick that had belonged to his grandmother.

He heard another noise from the direction of the kitchen to the back of the house. Gripping the walking stick tightly he carefully made his way down the passage and stopped at the kitchen door; light poured through the gap under it. Gently Gwyn placed his ear to the door and listened. He heard the scrape of a chair on the tiled floor and then the light went off, followed by the sound of the back door closing.

Taking a deep breath Gwyn opened the door and stepped into the kitchen. He immediately switched the light on and held the walking stick in the air ready to strike any burglars who might still have been inside.

The room was empty. His heart racing, Gwyn heard another sound: the tell-tale squeak of the garden gate.

He quickly ran back upstairs and into his bedroom. Without putting the light on he drew back the blackout curtain and looked down on the back alley. There was just enough of a moon for him to see a figure in a hat and coat walking away; it looked like his Uncle Keith.

Gwyn let out a huge sigh of relief. His uncle must have popped home for something. He felt a little foolish for getting so scared and thinking of burglars. Since the war there had been very little crime – local people had become a lot more caring towards one another.

After returning downstairs to get his glass of water Gwyn climbed into bed once more and closed his eyes. He began listing the full names of aeroplanes to help ease his mind so he could sleep: Hawker Hurricane, Supermarine Spitfire, Avro Lancaster … then after a while, when he still hadn't got to sleep, he started on German planes – they were more difficult – Heinkel He 111, Fokker G.1 'Reaper', Junkers Ju 87 'Stuka', Messerschmitt Bf 109 …

'Get up, Gwyn!'

Gwyn was roughly shaken from a dark dream in which he was roaming the desert calling out for his father.

'Gwyn! Get to the shelter quickly. I'll get your mother and sister.' Standing above his bed was Uncle Keith.

'What's happening?' asked Gwyn, still full of sleep.

'It's an air raid. Now go!'

Gwyn was suddenly wide awake. He jumped out of bed and began looking for his clothes.

'Hurry, boy!'

'I need to dress.'

'There's no time for that – just take your dressing gown and run.' Gwyn quickly put his dressing gown on over his pyjamas and followed Uncle Keith out of the room.

'What's going on?' called out his mother, waking up with the commotion.

'It's an air raid, Mrs Lazenby,' answered Uncle Keith. 'We need to get everyone to the shelter at once. Is Molly with you? Her bed is empty.'

'My goodness. Yes. She's with me.'

Uncle Keith waited on the landing while Gwyn's mother got out of bed and struggled into an overcoat which had been purposely left on a chair. Gwyn, who had refused to go on ahead, watched anxiously as Uncle Keith picked up his little sister in his arms.

'I want Rosie,' called out Molly.

Gwyn looked down at the bed and located his sister's rag doll. 'Here you are, Moll; now hold on tight, we're going to spend the night in our new den in the garden.'

The air raid siren began to scream out over the town. Gwyn looked at his uncle. 'How did you know there was an air raid? The sirens are only just going off.'

'I've just come back from work and heard the planes. Now quickly, we really must go!'

Uncle Keith led the way downstairs and into the kitchen.

'Wait,' called out Gwyn's mother, heading towards the pantry. 'Now what?!'

'There's the week's rations in there, we should take them with us.'

'Just leave them,' called back Uncle Keith in exasperation. 'Food is no good if you're dead.'

Out in the garden the air was filled with the drone of aeroplanes and the thump, thump of the anti-aircraft guns; the flashes of explosions punctuated the night sky in a deadly display of pyrotechnics.

Gwyn ran down the garden and stumbled over a row of potatoes in the darkness. He looked up and saw a shadowy box shape, and immediately recognised the chicken coop. 'Vera and Gracie!' he thought, catching his breath. 'I can't leave you girls out here,' he said. He reached inside the old tea chest, felt a bundle of feathers, and pulled one of the startled birds out. He tucked her under his arm, before retrieving the second, who was clucking in annoyance at being dragged from her cosy bed. 'Come on, girls, let's get out of here!' he said.

The sky to his right suddenly lit up with a huge flash, and an ear-splitting sound filled Gwyn with renewed terror. Running at full pelt he reached the shelter, and practically fell inside the door in a bundle of feathers. He immediately let out a yell as his feet sank into a pool of cold, muddy water; it had rained that day. He released the birds, and they fluttered to the top bunk, startling everyone in the shelter. 'What *are* you doing, Gwyn?' demanded his mother.

'I couldn't just leave them!' answered Gwyn. 'Besides, I like my eggs too much,' he joked bravely.

Molly was sitting on her mother's lap on the bottom bunk. She was crying; it was all too much for the little girl. Gwyn climbed up to the top bunk, while Uncle Keith made sure the shelter's door was firmly shut. Then he lit a candle and sat down on a wooden crate next to the door, with his feet resting against the wall.

There was just enough room for the four of them. The candlelight gave an eerie glow to their faces and their shadows danced on the walls in a silent puppet show.

'Rosie!' cried out Molly, suddenly.

'Where's her doll?' asked Gwyn's mother. 'Did she bring it with her?'

'Yes,' said Gwyn, 'I handed it to her in the house. Isn't it on the bunk?'

A quick search of the shelter drew a blank. 'She must have dropped it on the way here,' said Gwyn. 'Shall I go and look for it?'

'Don't be a fool,' said Uncle Keith. 'It will have to wait until the all clear.'

Sitting back down Gwyn felt helpless as his little sister sobbed quietly into her mother's shoulder.

'Let's sing a song, shall we?' suggested Gwyn's mother in an attempt to distract Molly. She cleared her throat and launched into an old song Gwyn had heard many times in the Palace Theatre music hall since the war had begun. 'It's a long way to Tipperary; it's a long way to go …' Gwyn joined in but Uncle Keith remained silent, apparently more interested in keeping one ear to the door.

Gradually a new sound arose above their singing: a series of high-pitched whistling sounds followed by loud thuds and explosions.

'It's the bombs,' said Uncle Keith reading Gwyn's thoughts. The singing abruptly stopped and they held their breath, listening to the noises getting closer and closer.

'They fall in clusters of four,' said Uncle Keith quietly.

Gwyn's mother began to pray out loud. Gwyn shut his eyes tightly and counted.

'One.'

'Two.'

'Three.'

The fourth was the loudest whistle of the night. It was a frightening screeching sound which grew in intensity. Instinctively they all ducked, believing a large bomb was about to score a direct hit on their shelter. The sound was suddenly replaced by an almighty thud. Then silence.

Gwyn opened his eyes again and looked around. His mother's eyes were still tightly shut and she was hugging the life out of Molly. Uncle Keith looked worried.

'That sounded like a high-explosive bomb,' he said.

'An H-E? But there was no explosion,' said Gwyn, puzzled.

Uncle Keith was busy thinking. Finally he made a decision.

'I'm going out to have a look.'

'But Mr Jenkins, it's too dangerous,' gasped Gwyn's mother. 'You said so yourself.'

'It would be more dangerous to sit here if there's a bomb about to go off right outside. Now don't worry, I'll be careful. Gwyn, come and close the door after me, there's a good boy.'

Gwyn climbed down from his bunk and waited for Uncle Keith to open the door. He watched him disappear from sight up the sloping trench and then closed the door once more. He sat on the crate and waited. The noise of the guns and aeroplanes seemed to be moving further away. After a few minutes Gwyn heard a knock on the door and he opened it again to see Uncle Keith standing outside.

'Did you find anything?' asked Gwyn's mother.

'No. Whatever it was must have landed somewhere else, but I am going to need your help, Gwyn, there's a few fires that need putting out.'

'Fires?' declared Gwyn's mother in alarm.

'Nothing too serious, Mrs Lazenby,' said Uncle Keith, 'they're only small, and it looks like the bombing is concentrated on the other side of town for now, but we don't want them to spread or attract any more attention.'

'You be careful, Gwyn,' warned his mother in a scared voice.

'I will, Mam.'

'Follow me and watch where you're putting your feet,' his uncle instructed.

Despite the danger Gwyn felt a sudden surge of excitement. He was surprised to find it was quite light outside, despite it being the middle of the night; then he realised the brightness was caused by fire. He heard the roar of flames, and the smell of burning filled his nostrils. A house in the next street was ablaze. The shouts of wardens and firemen rang out as they bravely tackled the burning building. It was just one of many buildings across Swansea to suffer such a fate that night.

Thankfully their house was untouched, for now at least, but there were three small fires in the garden.

'Incendiary bombs,' yelled Uncle Keith above the noise. 'They're designed to cause fires and light up the target area. We must put them out before they spread.'

'I'll get some water,' Gwyn called back.

'No. That will only spread the phosphorus. We'll have to use sand.'

Gwyn and his uncle carried a sandbag each from the shelter's entrance and dropped them close to the first fire, which was burning brightly in the middle of the vegetable patch.

Uncle Keith withdrew a frightening-looking knife, which Gwyn had not seen before, from his coat pocket, and stabbed it into one of the sandbags. He then slit it open and with Gwyn's help emptied the sand onto the fire. The heat was almost unbearable, and the thick smoke made Gwyn cough and splutter as the wind danced the flames around.

The fire was killed and they moved on to the next, which was near the outhouse at the bottom of the garden. 'Look!' exclaimed Gwyn catching sight of something on the roof in the light of the flickering flames. Lodged in some broken tiles was an unexploded incendiary bomb. It was about 2 feet long and 3 inches in diameter with fins on one end.

'Well spotted, Gwyn. If that goes off we'll lose the building.'

Looking around, Uncle Keith saw a broom resting next to the door. He picked it up and reached with the handle in an attempt to dislodge the device.

'It's no good. I can't reach.'

'Let me go on your shoulders,' begged Gwyn.

Gripping the broom tightly Gwyn climbed up on Uncle Keith's shoulders and they moved into position. Holding onto the guttering with one hand for balance, Gwyn stretched out with his other arm and pushed the broom handle under the bomb's fins. It moved a little and then, with another prod, the device fell loose and rolled to the ground.

The two turned their faces away, but fortunately the bomb didn't go off. They then collected more sandbags and covered the device in case it ignited.

The remaining fires were extinguished and they drew a smoky breath. 'Good work,' said Uncle Keith. 'Now let's get back into the shelter before another wave comes'. As they turned to go Gwyn saw a familiar little face on the ground: it was Molly's rag doll.

'Just look at the state of you,' said his mother, once Gwyn was safely back inside the shelter.

Gwyn looked down at himself. The arms of his dressing gown were singed and he had a few minor burns where the flames had licked against his hands. He was black with soot, his eyes streamed with tears caused by the smoke, and his throat felt dry and raw – but the fires were out.

Suddenly Gwyn remembered the doll in his pocket and pulled it out. 'Look, Molly, I found a friend of yours.'

Molly squealed with delight and hugged her doll tightly. Then taking a drink of cold tea from his mother, Gwyn climbed into his bunk. No one spoke. The excitement and tension of the night had drained all the words out of them. Finally, one by one, they began to drift off to sleep, shattered by their terrifying ordeal.

Gwyn heard Vera clucking, and opened his eyes to find her perched on his chest. Gracie was mooching around by his feet. 'I'm dreaming,' he thought, before the events of the previous night came back to him. The boy looked down from his bunk in time to see Uncle Keith stir, open his eyes, and look at his watch.

'It's gone 8 o'clock,' he said. 'Better shake a leg and see if we have a house left.' He woke the others, and they climbed out of the shelter. The sunlight made them blink. Smoke still clung to the air and from the distance they could hear the sound of emergency crews still fighting fires or rescuing people from collapsed buildings across the town.

Molly escaped her mother's hand and ran to the vegetable patch. 'Look, Mummy, there's a rabbit hole in the garden,' she called out pointing to an opening in the ground.

They all looked down and saw a hole about four feet in diameter in the ground next to the shelter.

'Right. I want everyone to slowly walk away and make their way into the street,' said Uncle Keith calmly. 'Gwyn, will you go next door and tell them to quietly leave their home as well? I'll tell the neighbours the other side.'

'But whatever's the matter?' asked Gwyn's mother.

'I think Molly may have solved the mystery of the vanishing fourth bomb,' answered Uncle Keith.

They had all had a lucky escape. If the bomb had gone off it would have taken their garden, house and shelter up with it, and they wouldn't have stood a chance.

A bomb disposal team was summoned and the street evacuated. The families made their way to a nearby church hall which had become an emergency centre. Cups of tea were handed out and volunteers tried to make everyone comfortable. Much to his displeasure Gwyn was given a change of clothes and then packed off to school.

'Just because Hitler drops a few bombs it doesn't mean your education suffers,' his mother ruled.

Chapter 4

A precious souvenir

Gwyn found it impossible to concentrate during lessons that day. Would the bomb be defused safely? Would he still have a home to go to after school? Thoughts of doom swirled around his head, and on more than one occasion the schoolmaster had to reprimand him for not paying attention.

On the final bell Gwyn couldn't get out of the school doors quickly enough. Closely followed by Owen, he raced back to the church hall, where a volunteer with a clipboard told Gwyn his mother and sister had been allowed to return home.

'That's good news, the bomb must have been defused,' said Owen helpfully.

The two boys ran through the streets only stopping to stare at the smouldering ruins of the house Gwyn had seen in flames the previous night. An ARP warden was standing guard at the gate.

'Did everyone get out?' asked Gwyn.

The warden gave a sad shake of the head. 'A whole family of six bought it. A direct hit. Didn't stand a chance.'

Gwyn looked down at his feet and realised he was standing in a stream of dirty-black water which was running out of the remains of the house. He watched the water collect in a puddle in the road where a girl's rag doll, quite similar to Molly's, lay face down. Gwyn picked it up, gave it a wipe and sat it on the garden wall of the ruined house.

'I should imagine she will come back for it,' he said not believing it himself. The ARP warden looked sad.

'Damn Germans!' Owen cursed out loud.

Gwyn looked away from the water to his friend and then looked at the warden, who didn't flinch. Usually a child would get a good ticking off for swearing.

The bomb disposal team, soldiers from the Royal Engineers, had dug a huge hole in the garden, shored up by planks of wood, to reach the bomb. An officer was talking to Gwyn's mother by the back door, while two cheery-looking soldiers were relaxing on a pile of freshly-dug earth.

'Hello,' said one of the soldiers on seeing Gwyn and Owen. 'Come to see Swansea's newest mine shaft?'

'Is it safe?' stammered Gwyn peering over the edge of the hole.

'Well, we wouldn't be lazing about if there was a ticking bomb under our feet,' laughed the other soldier, who reminded Gwyn of Ioan, one of his distant cousins, who was nineteen and in the Merchant Navy.

'Do you live here?' asked the first soldier.

'Yes, sir,' replied Gwyn.

'Easy on the sir, I ain't no officer,' said the soldier in mock horror; he then threw a piece of metal to Gwyn. 'Here, catch. A little souvenir for you.'

Gwyn and Owen looked at the strange object. 'What is it?' asked Owen.

'It's a fin from the bomb, pretty rare, I should imagine. You don't get to see many of those in one piece!'

Gwyn stared at the object in his hands.

'If you ask me that's worth its weight in gold to you.'

'How's that?' asked Gwyn puzzled.

'Because that bomb must have had your names on it to fall so close. You've cheated death, my boy.'

Gwyn thanked the soldiers and took the prized possession up

33

to his bedroom. On top of his chest of drawers sat a live bullet, and several pieces of shrapnel from anti-aircraft shells.

Gwyn sat on his bed and took a penknife out of his pocket and started scratching away at the bomb's fin.

'What are you doing?' asked Owen.

'I'm carving our names on it, just to make sure. I'll add yours too, if you want.'

'*Na*, it doesn't make any bones with me. I ain't afraid of no German bomb. If they want me they can try and take me, but it will be one hell of a fight.'

When Gwyn arrived down for breakfast the next morning there was an envelope sitting on the kitchen table. He sat down and saw his name, 'Master Gwyn Lazenby', written in a familiar handwriting that made his heart leap. He immediately turned to his mother with a grin almost the size of Swansea Bay.

'It's just arrived,' she smiled back.

'Can I read it now?'

'Eat your breakfast first, then you can take it into the parlour to have a bit of peace and quiet.'

Gwyn wolfed down his precious boiled egg (ever since the bombing began Vera and Gracie had almost given up laying) before snatching the letter up and bolting from the table.

'Where's your manners?' shouted his mother, 'You're nothing more than a sand boy!'

Gwyn grinned – his mother always called him that when she was pretending to be cross with him, though he had no idea what a 'sand boy' was! 'Excuse me!' he shouted back from down the passage before disappearing into the front room, which was kept for special occasions such as Sunday lunches and entertaining visitors.

Gwyn sat at a finely-carved wooden bureau and reached into

a drawer to pull out a letter knife. He pushed the blade into the top corner of the envelope and ever so carefully opened it up. It was dated six weeks earlier but Gwyn was used to the slow delivery of letters. It was a fact of wartime life. His fingers were shaking slightly as he unfolded the letter and began to read:

Dear Gwyn,

I hope you are well and working hard in school and being good for your mother. Myself, I am in good health and still in one piece despite having a few run-ins with Jerry, but me and the boys gave a good account of ourselves so don't worry.

We are stationed in the desert at the moment and busy training for a new push which could make a real difference. We are all very excited and feel proud to have been selected for this job ▄▄▄▄▄▄▄▄▄▄▄▄

The next part was blocked out in thick black ink. Gwyn knew that the letter had been censored by a commanding officer. Gwyn read around the missing words trying to work out what they said. He understood the army had to be careful that valuable information didn't fall into the wrong hands, but he was desperate to know where his father was. It was terrible listening to news of battles on the wireless without knowing if he had been involved or not.

Feeling a little disappointed he read on:

I have sent you a picture of me and my chums, as you can see I am very much alive although a little skinnier, the army food is nothing like your mother's!

Gwyn looked inside the envelope and found the photograph. He studied it carefully. His father was standing in front of a jeep in the desert with three of his mates. They were all smiling and looked very brown in their short sleeves and khaki shorts. At that moment Gwyn had never missed his father so much.

He returned to the letter.

> *I have put in for some leave but can not say when I will be home, as I have said I think they have big plans for the regiment.*
>
> *Work hard in school and look after your mother and sister for me and keep out of trouble. I miss you all very much, God willing all this will be over soon and we can be a proper family once again.*
>
> *All the best all the time,*
> *Dad.*

Gwyn read it through once more and wondered what special mission his father had been selected for.

In the beginning Gwyn had thought his Dad being in the army was exciting and he was thrilled when his father had first come home on leave in his uniform. He had tried the jacket and hat on and shot imaginary Germans on the stairs, but these days the boy had a greater understanding of the reality of war. He only had to remember Owen's tear-stained face after learning his father had been killed in the retreat from France to know it was far from being a game.

Putting the letter and photograph carefully back into the envelope Gwyn stood up and looked out of the window. It was a clear sunny day and he could see children playing in the street.

Gwyn decided to venture outside and stood on the front step

watching two small boys chase each other with their toy aeroplanes, mimicking the sound of a dog fight.

'Eeerrrrrrmmmmmmmm, ack, ack, ack!'

It sounded quite a battle.

His little sister Molly was wheeling Rosie down the middle of the road in her little pram. Gwyn gave her a wave. She was quite safe, because with petrol being rationed there was hardly any traffic on the side streets.

Gwyn was about to sit back down again when he heard another sound which sent a chill down his spine ... it was the sound of a real aeroplane, but not with an engine sound he recognised.

He ran to the front door in time to see a German fighter skimming the roof tops. It rose into the sky and made a sweeping turn before homing in on their street. The aeroplane levelled off and suddenly opened up its guns, sending a shower of bullets tearing into the road and ripping up the tarmac in puffs of smoke.

'Look out!' Gwyn yelled.

The boys scarpered for cover but to his horror Gwyn saw Molly standing like a statue, staring up at the aeroplane, which was headed straight towards her.

Uncle Keith said afterwards that until someone is caught up in a life-threatening situation, you never know how they are going to react. The papers, he said, were full of stories of people who had either crumpled or risen to the challenge.

It was true.

Gwyn sprinted into the road and without slowing down swept Molly up in his arms. Ahead of him was a doorway between two bow windows belonging to a bakery. The uneven weight of his sister made him stumble and his ankle gave way. Just as he thought they would end up in a heap in the road Gwyn somehow found the strength to regain his balance and dive head-first into the shop doorway. The aeroplane screeched closer making a sound like a hundred motorcars revving their engines. At the same time bullets slammed into the building with a series of hissing thuds, shattering its windows and sending bits of wood and stone flying in the air.

The sound of the aeroplane reached an ear-splitting level as it passed overhead. Gwyn was so full of adrenalin he didn't feel the hard floor or the solid door which stopped their slide. He curled up into a ball, wrapping his body around Molly.

The whole world seemed to stand still in a bubble of silence. Gwyn was suddenly aware of his heart beating furiously. He lay still, listening to the sound of the plane growing fainter, and then felt Molly struggling to free herself from his tight grasp. He blinked open his eyes. It was like waking from a dream. He was shocked to see Molly's doll's pram lying on its side, shredded by the plane's bullets.

'I want my Mummy,' she cried.

'It's okay, Moll,' said Gwyn soothingly, sitting up. 'Mam's only over the road.'

The pair were covered in bits of debris but amazingly, apart from a few bumps and bruises, they appeared to have escaped serious injury. The brickwork of the doorway had saved them.

Gwyn looked out across the street to see the children staring back open-mouthed. Then he saw his mother hurtling out of their house. She ran, with her apron swinging from side to side, across the street and fell to her knees in the doorway. She smothered them both with a huge hug and kissed them repeatedly, faster than the shower of bullets from earlier.

'My babies, my babies!' she cried.

By now all the neighbours were out and Gwyn and Molly were helped to their feet. One old man shook a fist to the sky shouting out, 'Come down here and fight like a man!' Then he turned to the others in the street. 'Nazi dogs! They must have seen they were only children playing.'

Once Gwyn and Molly were safely back inside their home Mrs Lazenby insisted on putting them both to bed until the doctor arrived to give them a proper examination. Gwyn sat upright while his mother tucked the eiderdown around him tightly.

'Drink that sweet tea I made you,' she said. 'You may be in shock.'

'Is there anything that you can't cure by drinking tea?' Gwyn asked looking at the cup by the side of his bed.

'Now don't you give me any cheek, hero or not, my boy. This family has always sworn by its tea. It's the British way,' answered his mother before planting a big kiss on his forehead.

'Aww, Mam! What was that for?'

'For being so brave,' she answered before wiping a tear from the corner of her eye. 'Now rest, I'm going to see to your sister.'

Gwyn suddenly realised how tired he was. His body felt drained of energy and his ankle was sore. Alone in his room he thought back to what had just happened. He still could not believe it. Then his mind began to ask questions. What if he had been too late? He tried to shake off the thought. Molly was safe in bed, he had saved her. They were both safe. But for how long, he began to think. He started to wish that he and his whole family could move out of Swansea, away from the bullets and bombs.

Gwyn must have fallen asleep, because the next time he opened his eyes Dr Thomas was standing over him.

'Well, young man, let's see how you are after your little adventure, shall we?'

'How's Molly?' Gwyn immediately asked.

'Don't you worry, she's right as rain,' the doctor replied, 'thanks to you, by all accounts. Now open your pyjama top, there's a good boy.'

The doctor took a stethoscope out from his black bag and listened to Gwyn's chest. 'That's normal,' he said before taking the boy's temperature and blood pressure. Satisfied with the results he put his instruments back into the bag. 'Now then, are you in any pain at all?'

'Just my ankle, it's a bit sore,' answered Gwyn.

'Let's take a look.'

The doctor held Gwyn's ankle in both hands.

'Does that hurt at all?' he asked, putting pressure on the joint.

'A little bit,' replied Gwyn, biting his lip.

'Can you move your foot in a circle for me?'

Gwyn did as he was asked, but the movement felt uncomfortable. He looked down to see a massive bruise around his ankle.

'Mmmm. It looks like you may have sprained it,' the doctor said. 'I don't think he needs an X-ray,' he continued, looking at Gwyn's mother, who was standing anxiously by the door. 'A few days' bed rest should do the trick.'

'Thank you, Dr Thomas. I'm sure he won't mind missing school for a while,' answered Gwyn's mother .

'Oh, and take one of these four times a day,' the doctor smiled, handing Gwyn a small paper bag containing boiled sweets.

'Wow!' exclaimed Gwyn, 'I didn't know you could still get these!'

'Only for medical emergencies,' laughed back Dr Thomas.

'Thank you so much, doctor,' said Gwyn's mother.

'My pleasure, Mrs Lazenby, it's not every day I get to treat a hero.' The doctor ruffled Gwyn's hair and was shown out.

That evening Gwyn was allowed downstairs for his tea. He sat in his father's chair next to the range in the kitchen with his bad leg resting on an old cushion on the coal scuttle. His mother busied herself with preparing the meal. She placed a bowl of dripping on the large wooden table and then returned with a jar of pickled onions and a small lump of cheese. She then started slicing a loaf of bread.

Molly was sitting at the table drawing on a piece of cardboard while happily singing to herself. She appeared none the worse for her ordeal.

Uncle Keith was also at the table going through his reporter's notebook. Gwyn had often wondered at the strange marks and scribbles that made up the shorthand. His uncle had tried to teach him the basics but it was like a strange coded language to Gwyn.

There was a knock on the door. 'I'll get it,' said Uncle Keith, climbing to his feet and opening the door. 'Ah, Howell, good, you got my message. Please come in,' he said. Gwyn recognised Howell Evans, the ancient but friendly photographer from the newspaper.

Uncle Keith turned to Gwyn's mother, 'Mrs Lazenby, I hope you don't mind but I thought we could get a picture of Gwyn and Molly for the paper. I'm going to write a little piece on how Gwyn saved his sister.'

Gwyn's mother stopped cutting the loaf and thought for a few seconds before answering. 'I don't know, Mr Jenkins, you know what I think about that gossip rag of yours.'

'Mrs Lazenby, this is not gossip, it's fact, it really happened. Now don't you think people have a right to know about it?'

'Well, as long as Gwyn is happy with the idea, I suppose it can't do any harm. But he's to change out of those school clothes and into his Sunday best if his picture's going in the paper.'

Uncle Keith turned to Gwyn, 'What do you think, Gwyn? Do you want to be headline news?'

'Do I!' returned Gwyn, his face full of excitement. He could just imagine the looks he would get when he returned to school. He might even get a mention in assembly.

'Off you go to the bathroom then, my boy,' said Gwyn's mother. 'You too, Molly, let's get you nice and tidy.' She marched Molly upstairs, Gwyn hobbling behind. For a moment Gwyn regretted saying 'yes' as his mother made sure his face was scrubbed clean. 'When was the last time you had a proper wash? There's enough dirt behind your ears to grow potatoes,' she cried.

A little while later Gwyn was sitting in his shirt and tie with his face glowing and hair slicked neatly to one side. Molly, wearing her best floral dress and a pink cardigan, and her hair in bunches, sat on her brother's lap.

'Now give your sister a big *cwtch*,' called out Howell, 'That's it, put her cheek next to yours. That's lovely.'

There was a big flash and the picture was taken. Both Gwyn and Molly rubbed their eyes, almost blinded by the sudden bright light.

'Now, Mr Evans, would you care to join us for some supper?'

'That would be wonderful, Mrs Lazenby. I've been non-stop all day and haven't had time to eat yet.'

'That doesn't sound like the reporter's life to me.'

'Ah, well now, things aren't as easy as they used to be. With the war on the staff's down to the bare bones, and two-hour lunches are a thing of the past, thanks to Mr Hitler. And not all of us get to have a day off like Keith here.'

'I more than make up for it when I'm in work, don't you worry,' chipped in Uncle Keith helping himself to a smear of dripping for his bread. 'What's the lead story for tomorrow, anyway?'

'Haven't you heard? There's a big hunt for a spy over in St Thomas.'

Uncle Keith put his bread down and looked at the photographer. 'A spy?'

'Yes, a spy. It seems he, well, I suppose it could be a she, was spotted signalling a German plane from Kilvey Hill late last night.'

Gwyn sat up in his chair and looked across open-mouthed at Uncle Keith.

'What type of signalling?' Uncle Keith asked.

'A torch, they think. One of the Home Guard saw a series of flashes just when a plane was flying over.'

Uncle Keith asked, 'Did they see who it was?' Gwyn thought his voice was a bit sharp, and thought how worried he sounded.

'*Na*, not yet. They've searched but got nothing. The police want us to print an appeal for people to come forward if they think they know something.'

'But why would a spy be in Swansea?' asked Gwyn.

'Well, Swansea is an important port, not to mention the big oil storage tanks in Llandarcy and the ammunition factories,' pointed out the friendly old photographer.

'It's madness,' Uncle Keith said suddenly. 'They'll get all sorts of people with a grievance against someone else making up allegations just to get them in trouble.'

'All the same,' replied Howell, 'if there's a German spy in our midst something must be done about it.'

Uncle Keith stood up. 'Are you heading back to the *Post* now?'

'Yes, I've got to get this picture developed.'

'I'll come with you then,' he replied, getting his coat, before adding, 'I may as well set Gwyn's story out myself, just to make sure it's not changed. I don't want Mrs Lazenby throwing me out.' A smile returned to his face and he winked at Gwyn before following his colleague out of the door.

Molly climbed off her chair and snuggled onto her mother's lap.

'Mummy, what's a spy?' she asked.

'It's a baddy, my little flower.'

'Is he going to get us?' she returned, her eyes opening wide in alarm.

'Don't be silly, you've got your big brave brother and Uncle Keith to look after you.'

Gwyn finished his supper quietly. Not only was the enemy sending aeroplanes to attack his town, but now there was a real live German spy living amongst them.

Chapter 5

Dreadful news

Gwyn spent the next three days confined to the house. He had been thrilled to see his picture and story on an inside page of the newspaper, with the headline 'Boy Saves Sister From Cowardly Attack', but he was desperately bored. When he was finally allowed out he headed straight for Owen's house a few streets away.

As Gwyn entered the passageway leading to the back of Owen's home he was greeted by a big black and white cat tearing towards him. It let out a loud, startled meow and was quickly followed by Owen who almost knocked Gwyn over.

'Steady, Owe, I've only just recovered from being shot up,' said Gwyn, holding his hands out to stop his friend.

'Sorry, Gwyn, I was trying to catch Snowy.'

'Snowy?' answered Gwyn. 'But Snowy is white, that moggie was black and white ... come to think about it, the front half was black and the back half white. That's pretty unusual for a cat.'

'That's because it *is* Snowy. I'm trying to paint him black.'

Gwyn stared at Owen, then noticed his hands, too, were black. He held them up for Gwyn to see. 'It's blacklead, the stuff you use on the fireplace.'

'But why on earth would you want to do something like that to poor old *Snowy*?' asked Gwyn in disbelief.

'It's a long story, but if I don't my mum is going to have him drowned.'

'Drowned?' asked Gwyn, still none the wiser.

'Yes, drowned, because she doesn't want to get bombed.'

'You've completely lost me now. You sure you haven't got a piece of shrapnel in your head or something?'

'I better start again,' said Owen. 'Come on, I'll show you.'

The two boys walked through the passage and sat on a bench in the back garden. Owen pointed to the family's air raid shelter. 'Every time we go to the shelter at night the blinking cat comes along and sits on top. He never comes inside, hates it down there, but always sits on top.'

'What's so bad about that?' asked Gwyn.

'Hey, I thought you were supposed to be the one with all the brains. What colour is he? Let's think now, he's called *Snowy*,' said Owen deliberately, looking hard at Gwyn.

Gwyn suddenly got it. 'Oh my goodness, a big white cat marking your shelter.'

'Mam is convinced the Germans will spot him and drop a big bomb on us.'

'But why colour him black, why not just lock him in the house?'

'Oh, he'll get out somehow, we're hardly going to have time to close all the windows in a raid.'

'Well, I suppose it's better than being put to sleep,' said Gwyn with a smile.

The two friends shared a laugh before Owen became serious again. 'I hate this war,' he said.

'Me too. I wish it would all end, so much.'

Owen took a quick look around before saying in a lowered voice, 'There's something I want to show you, but it's top secret. You have to swear not to tell anyone.'

'I swear. Where is it?'

'It's upstairs, but we'll have to be careful Mam doesn't see us. She should be popping out soon to check on our neighbour. I'll show you then.'

'This is all very mysterious,' replied Gwyn, 'What's it all about?'

'It's about fighting back.'

'Against who?' asked Gwyn.

'The Germans, of course. They killed my father, they are dropping bombs all over the place, and now they try to machine-gun you and little Molly in the street.'

Gwyn knew his friend wasn't joking. It was just like Owen to do something brave and rash. He had always been a bit crazy, but since his father's death Owen seemed to go out of his way to get into trouble. Once he had thrown a glass bottle across the school yard for no reason at all. Gwyn had been surprised his friend had only received a telling-off and not the cane.

'But what can we do?' asked Gwyn.

Just then Owen's mother came out of the back door.

She smiled at Gwyn. 'Hello, Gwyn, I'm glad to see you are up and about. Terrible business with that plane, I read all about it in the paper. Give my regards to your mother for me.'

'I will, Mrs Jones, thank you,' answered Gwyn.

Mrs Jones smiled. 'Owen, I shouldn't be too long, just checking on old Mr Edwards.'

The boys watched her disappear. Then Owen grabbed Gwyn's arm.

'Come on, I'll show you.'

He led his friend into the house and upstairs into the main bedroom. Owen picked up a chair and placed it next to the wardrobe. Standing on the seat he reached up on top and lifted a long object wrapped in a piece of cloth.

'Here, grab this.'

He passed the rather heavy bundle to Gwyn, jumped down, and then took it back and placed it on the bed.

'What is it?' asked Gwyn.

Owen grabbed the cloth and pulled it up, revealing a double-barrelled shotgun.

'Blimey!' spluttered Gwyn. 'Where did that come from?'

'It was my grandfather's. He used it to shoot rats on his farm.

My father brought it with him when they sold up.'

Gwyn looked at the gun and ran his hand down the long barrels. It felt icy cold and gave him a little shiver. 'But weren't you supposed to hand guns over to the police when the war started?' he asked.

'My father said there was no way he was going to give up a family heirloom.' Owen picked the gun up and held it to his shoulder, aiming at the ceiling.

'Careful,' said Gwyn anxiously.

'It's okay, it's not loaded,' reassured his friend. 'But it will be when it comes to showing those Germans not to trifle with Swansea boys!'

Gwyn looked worried.

'So, are you in?' asked Owen, still looking along the barrel of the gun.

'I don't know. What are you going to do, stand in the street and start firing?'

'Why not? When Jerry flies past they can have both barrels.'

'I don't know, Owe. What if we get caught?'

'It's a risk I'm going to take. You've seen what they're doing to our town. Besides, during an air raid all you can hear is guns going off, no one will notice. We're at war. They're the enemy. We'll be sent off to fight when we are eighteen if it's still going on. Why wait, I say?'

Gwyn, not wanting to give an answer, asked, 'Have you got cartridges?'

'They're locked away in a drawer downstairs. So what's it going to be – are you in?'

Gwyn was afraid – not just of the danger, he also knew it was wrong. He daren't imagine what his Uncle Keith would say if they were caught.

'When are you doing it?' he asked.

'Tonight.'

'Tonight?' repeated Gwyn in amazement.

'Why not?'

'Well, you need to plan it all out, do some recce, find the best place to shoot from, and how will you explain to your mam why you're not in the shelter?'

The two boys were silent for a few moments before Owen said, 'Well, that's why I need your help, you're the one with the brains.'

'What about Tom? Have you asked him?'

'There's no point, he told me in school today he's being evacuated, sent away to live with his aunt.'

'That's terrible.'

Owen started to wrap the gun up again. 'So you're the only friend I really trust.'

'I don't know, Owe. I'll have to think about it.'

'Okay, but I'll need an answer soon, or I'll do it myself.'

Gwyn didn't doubt this. When Owen said he was going to do something he meant it.

Gwyn left Owen's house deep in thought. His friend's idea for revenge scared him, but a part of him wanted to join in, despite knowing it was wrong. Gwyn had always kept to the rules, he had never disobeyed his parents or got into trouble like some of the boys on his street. OK, so he got into mischief now and then in school, but who didn't? Then the memory of diving for cover amidst the shower of bullets and Molly's screams came back to him again. The world had changed. In Sunday School Gwyn had learnt the Ten Commandments. 'Thou shalt not kill' was one of them, yet good men were now doing exactly that. The rules had changed. People he knew, his father, his teacher Mr Williams, his neighbours, were away in foreign countries fighting for their freedom.

Still lost in thought, Gwyn left the houses behind and climbed a steep, grassy slope up to Townhill, which overlooked Swansea. Once on top he made for a bench where he liked to sit when he wanted to spend time alone.

He gazed out at the view. To the left lay the docks, with their rows of cranes busily lifting much-needed supplies out of the bellies of the large ships, many of which had been attacked by German U-boats during the crossing from America. Behind were the grey streets and rows of terrace houses of St Thomas, where the dock workers lived, banking their way up the slopes of Kilvey Hill, which stood watch over the east side of the town. On top Gwyn could just make out a gun battery with its sights trained on the Bristol Channel in readiness to take pot shots at the enemy when they came.

The Tawe wound its way down the valley and through the docks to the sea. On its west bank was the huge concrete Weaver's flour mill, and a little further on, the town centre. Gwyn could make out the tower of St Mary's church, the glass roof of the indoor market and the streets of fine Victorian buildings housing the once busy shops.

Gwyn was disturbed from his thoughts by a familiar voice. 'Room for one more?'

Gwyn turned around to see his friend Tom. He looked really sad, he had his hands in his pockets and was kicking his feet into the ground as he approached. 'Of course,' said Gwyn, giving his friend a smile as he moved along the bench. 'I heard about you being evacuated, that's rotten luck.'

'My mother told me yesterday. She said after the bombings and shootings me and my brother are going to live with our aunt in Carmarthen, away from the docks.'

A few of the children in Gwyn's school had been evacuated when the war first started but most had come back a few months later because there weren't any attacks. Now children were being sent to the safety of the countryside again. Gwyn had even heard Uncle Keith asking his mother if there was anywhere she could send Gwyn and Molly, but she had said the Germans weren't going to break her family up any further.

'Don't worry, Tom, it's not that far away, and at least you will be with people you know. I'm sure it won't be for long, and you can always come back and visit on the train,' said Gwyn trying to console his friend.

'That's if there's still a Swansea to come back to,' said Tom staring out across the town. 'And it's only me and Rob that's going. Mam won't come with us, says who'll look after the house?'

For once Gwyn didn't know what to say. He imagined how he would feel if he was sent away, worrying about his own mother sheltering from bombs each night.

The two boys sat in silence. Gwyn's eye followed a slow, clanking tram as it made its way along its tracks from the town centre, down St Helen's Road towards the Uplands and suburbia. Near the seafront itself were the Vetch Field and St Helens cricket ground, where the boys had stood in the crowd and cheered the Swans or Glamorgan on – it all seemed so long ago now.

'Tom, can I ask you something? But it's a secret.' Gwyn had decided to ask his advice on Owen's plan. The three had been close friends since they had first met in infants' school.

'Sounds exciting,' replied Tom, turning to look at his friend.

'You hate the Germans, right?'

'After what they are doing? Of course I do.'

'Yeah, but do you think it's right to shoot at them?' Gwyn told him all about Owen's plan and sat back to see what Tom suggested.

'I can see why he wants to do it,' said Tom after thinking deeply. 'If one of my family had been killed I don't know what I would do.

But it all sounds pretty dangerous to me. And if you get caught you are going to be in a whole heap of trouble.'

Gwyn thought carefully before asking, 'Yeah, but if you weren't going away would you come along?'

'I'm not sure. It's very risky, and have you stopped to think – if there is an air raid, you could end up getting killed!'

Gwyn hadn't really thought of that. How would his parents feel, and what would Molly do without her big brother to look after her?

'Whatever you decide, be careful,' said Tom rising to his feet. He held out his hand. 'I better be getting along, got to pack. I'm off in the morning, nine o'clock train.'

Gwyn shook his friend's hand warmly. 'I know you hate writing but drop us a letter if you get a chance and let us know how you're getting on.'

'I will,' replied Tom, getting up.

Gwyn watched sadly as his friend walked off. Soon he, too, got up to make his own way home. He was still no closer to making a decision when he arrived on his street, in time to see an important-looking army officer being shown out of his house by Uncle Keith. Gwyn stood to one side to allow the stony-faced soldier to walk out of the gate and climb into a car which was parked outside.

Uncle Keith stood in the doorway. His usually friendly face had a worried look on it. 'Gwyn, there's something I have to tell you,' he said.

'Where's my mother?'

'She's inside, but listen …'

Gwyn didn't wait to listen, he pushed past and ran into the kitchen. His mother was sitting at the table holding Molly on her lap. On hearing footsteps she looked up at Gwyn and tried to hide the fact she had been crying.

'What is it? Is it Dad?'

The tears began to flow again and Gwyn rushed to comfort his mother.

'What's happened?' he asked.

'He's missing,' his mother managed to blurt out between sobs.

Uncle Keith walked in and put his hand on Gwyn's shoulder. 'Now there's no need to fear the worst, he could turn up at any time.'

'But I only had a letter from him this week,' mumbled Gwyn in disbelief. 'When did it happen?'

'They didn't go into detail, they just said that your father is missing in action. Most probably during a mission behind enemy lines.'

Gwyn sat down and fell into silence. His world had been turned upside down. He looked at his mother's distraught face and Molly's confused eyes; then he thought of his father and tears silently ran down his cheeks. Finally his thoughts turned towards Owen, his shotgun and the crazy idea of fighting back.

Chapter 6

Gwyn makes up his mind

Gwyn watched his mother on her knees attacking the kitchen fireplace with blacklead. She had already scrubbed the large wooden table spotless.

'There will be nothing left of that grate by the time you're finished,' observed Gwyn.

'Mind your manners, my boy, it won't clean itself.'

Gwyn knew that this was just his mother's way of dealing with the bad news. Molly was too young to understand the situation. While Uncle Keith set about writing letters to the War Office, Gwyn's mother busied herself with the housework and put on a brave face. No one was allowed to give up hope or fear the worst; they were to carry on with their upturned lives as best they could. 'Easier said than done,' Gwyn told himself. He saw the reminders of loss everywhere in the town, from the burnt-out shells of houses, where whole families had perished, to the growing number of war-widows, who passed silently in the street, unable to come to terms with the death of their husbands in far-off battles.

Now Gwyn had revenge firmly on his mind and he was anxious to set his plan in motion. 'Is it all right if I go out for a while?' he asked his mother.

'Where are you going? I don't want you going too far from the house.' Gwyn had noticed his mother becoming a lot more anxious about his whereabouts of late.

'I won't be long, I've arranged to meet Owen. I'll be back in time for tea, promise.'

Ten minutes later Gwyn was sitting on his favourite bench on Townhill awaiting the arrival of Owen. He looked down on the view.

The town had already changed in the few days since he had said goodbye to Tom; even more gaps had appeared on the skyline, more buildings reduced to rubble. Swansea was in a mess and it was time for Gwyn and Owen to do their bit for the war effort.

Owen arrived up the hill panting for breath and plonked himself down on the bench. 'Sorry I'm late, I had to take my *brawd* to *Mam-gu*'s. What's so important that you have to drag me all the way up here anyway?'

'It's the best place to start planning,' answered Gwyn.

'Planning what?'

'Our date with Jerry.'

'You mean …'

'I'm in. I want some German blood on my hands.' Gwyn surprised himself with this last remark, but did not regret the growing desire for revenge.

'What made your mind up?' asked Owen. 'I'm not being funny but I didn't think you'd have it in you.'

Gwyn told Owen about the news of his father's disappearance. He tried not to sound too distressed because he knew that Owen had lost his own father for real. He didn't want to seem insensitive by talking about it and bringing the hurt to the surface.

'That's bad news, mun,' said Owen after Gwyn had finished, 'You can have first shot after that.'

Gwyn looked at his friend and admired how brave and fearless he always appeared to be.

'What's the plan then?'

Gwyn pointed to the view of the town, 'Take a look and tell me the best place to fire from.'

'What's wrong with right here?'

'Too many houses nearby; we'll get caught.'

Owen looked out across the town again and then smiled. 'Kilvey Hill,' he exclaimed, looking at the bare mountain to the east of the docks.

'Exactly! It's wild and craggy, with lots of heather for cover, and we'll get a great view of the planes when they make their runs.'

Owen gave Gwyn a slap on the back. 'Spot on, Master Lazenby, I knew there was some reason I keep you around.'

'The main problem though,' Gwyn carried on, 'is getting into position.'

'How do you mean?'

'Well, we've got to get across town, with the gun, without anyone seeing us. It will be easier after dark but not so easy in the blackout. Then there's the North Dock and the Tawe to negotiate.'

'What about the bridges?'

'They'll be guarded.'

'We could go up the valley and around the docks but we'll still have to cross the Tawe at some point.'

'Fine; we'll swim it then.'

Gwyn stared at his friend. 'In this weather?'

'Tough measures call for tough action.'

Gwyn shook his head, 'OK, but we'll have to work out a way of keeping the gun dry.'

'I'll leave that to you and your brains again.'

The boys sat in silence. Gwyn's attention was drawn to a grey ship steaming its way across the bay below, heading to the docks. 'Got it,' he announced. 'We'll build a little raft.'

'That will mean having to carry it across town.'

'No. We'll just take some empty cans and some string, we can collect some wood nearer the river and build it when we get there.'

'Well done,' said Owen. 'It's all coming together nicely.

'There is another problem,' said Gwyn.

'What?'

'We'll need to think about what we're going to tell our families.'

'That should be easy enough, you can tell your mother you're at my house and I'll tell mine I'm at yours … not that Mam gives a fig where I am these days.'

The boys sat in silence and looked out to sea. On a clear day you could see Devon from their vantage point; then, a few dozen miles the other side, lay the English Channel and a little further, German-occupied France. The enemy was closing in.

'I better be getting home,' said Gwyn eventually. 'We can talk about this tomorrow.'

'Hang on a minute, I've got an idea,' Owen replied.

Owen got up and made for a bombsite between two houses behind them. Gwyn followed and the two boys scrambled over the rubble.

'This should do,' said Owen hauling out a smashed-up kitchen table missing a couple of legs. 'Give us a hand to get this across the road.'

They placed the table upside-down on the grass near the top of the slope.

'What do you plan to do with this?' asked Gwyn puzzled.

'Ride it to the bottom, of course,' replied Owen. 'It beats walking.'

Gwyn looked at the slope which banked steeply down to a row of houses below. 'You're mad.'

'Come on, Gwyn, it will be fun; besides I want to find out if you've really got what it takes to join the mission. Call it an initiation test.'

'But we could break our necks.'

'And we could be blown up by a bomb at any minute. Live for today, I say.'

Owen pushed the table closer to the edge and sat down with his feet wedged against its wooden lip. 'Are you coming or what?' he asked impatiently.

Gwyn took another look at the slope before studying his friend's determined face; he was as serious as ever. Then he climbed on and sat behind Owen, gripping one of the remaining legs. If he was going to be a fighter it was time to start living dangerously, Gwyn told himself.

'Ready?'

'Ready,' Gwyn muttered, sounding far from convinced.

'Chocks away!'

The boys pushed the ground with their hands and rocked the table forwards. Slowly it edged closer to the drop. They pushed again. Suddenly the front end tipped forwards and gravity took over. Gwyn felt a rush of wind hit his face and an incredible sensation, a mixture of sheer exhilaration and potent fear, washed over him as they began accelerating downhill. Owen began whooping while Gwyn gritted his teeth and anxiously looked ahead at the onrushing houses.

Every now and then the table would hit a mound or clump of bracken, making them bump into the air before crashing back down again with an almighty jolt that threatened to throw them off.

'How do we stop?' cried Gwyn, realising they were running out of slope.

'I don't know!' came the unhelpful reply.

Just then the boys realised they were heading straight for a garden wall. 'Jump!' Owen yelled, throwing himself sideways.

Gwyn took a few seconds to realise he needed to take the same drastic action before being smashed to smithereens. Closing his eyes he bailed out to his left and immediately began rolling like an escaped wheel. As he bounced and slid he tried to grab at the long grass to slow himself down.

The table smashed into the stone wall with a terrific smack which sounded like a gun shot. Gwyn saw the wall racing towards him and cried out in panic before he felt a cold, wet sensation and began to slow down in a spray of muddy water: he had slid into a patch of bog.

He lay still, face down, and regained control of his breathing before looking up. 'Owen!' he shouted trying to locate his friend. He looked for the table, which lay split in two at the foot of the wall, but there was no sign of Owen.

Climbing unsteadily to his feet he called out again, 'Owen! Where are you?'

Then came a groan, followed by a shaky, 'I'm over here.'

Gwyn walked around a large bush to his right and saw Owen sticking out of a tangle of brambles. Gwyn pulled him free. Luckily he had gone in feet first, but his legs were badly scratched. The two sat back to draw breath.

'Perhaps it would be better to walk next time. If I still *can* walk, that is,' said Owen and the pair burst out laughing.

Gwyn lay back and stared up at the sky; the same sky under which they would soon be waiting for German bombers, armed and ready.

The Germans came again that night and Gwyn and his family spent a sleepless five hours or so huddled together in their shelter. Fortunately the seemingly endless drone of aeroplane engines passed overhead without too much excitement. The bombing appeared to have been centred on the other side of town, with few close calls, as had happened on the previous raid.

By dawn the 'all clear' had sounded, and after a hurried breakfast of bread and powdered milk, Gwyn reluctantly left for another day of school – or so he thought! As he turned the corner of De-La Beche Street to head up Mount Pleasant to the Grammar School he saw Owen running down the steep hill towards him, waving his hands excitedly in the air.

'What's the matter?' asked Gwyn, as he waited for his friend to get his breath back.

'No school today!' grinned Owen. 'Or for quite a while, I should imagine.'

'Why? What's up?'

'What's up? The school's up, that's what! Blown to kingdom come.'

'No!'

'Yes! A direct hit!'

Gwyn knew he shouldn't really be pleased; nevertheless, he felt a rush of excitement. He grabbed Owen's shoulders and the pair of them jumped up and down in a little dance.

After running to the school to take a look for himself, Gwyn invited Owen back to his house, where they told his mother the news.

'Good gracious!' she exclaimed. 'What's going to happen to your education now?'

'They will arrange something or other,' said Gwyn.

'But not for a week or so,' Owen grinned.

'You don't have to seem too pleased with yourselves,' she scolded gently.

'We're not, Mam, honest,' said Gwyn, trying not to sound too cheerful.

'Well, you could have fooled me. Now, make yourself useful, as you're here, and go and tidy the shelter. There's feathers everywhere, thanks to those blessed chickens.'

After taking the bedding out of the Anderson shelter and giving it a good shake the boys stood on top of the shelter, gazing over to the town centre where smoke was lingering in the sky, when Gwyn's mother called and asked them to run an errand for her. In his tiredness Uncle Keith had rushed off to work without any food. Now they were safely back inside their home she had made some lunch for her lodger and wanted Gwyn to deliver it to the *Evening Post* office in the town centre. The boys readily agreed, as it would give them an opportunity to survey the latest bomb damage.

'You be careful, mind you. If you hear the sirens going off make sure you head straight to the nearest shelter,' she warned.

The *Evening Post* offices were next to the old ruins of Swansea Castle, near the town's North Dock. Gwyn and Owen walked down Oxford Street and passed the remains of the indoor market. The stone walls and elegant entrance façade were still standing, but the huge glass roof had collapsed in on itself in a pile of twisted metal after being hit by several incendiary bombs.

The traders had been devastated to find their market-place destroyed but they had set up stalls on the pavement instead. The boys looked on enviously at an old woman in a shawl selling cockles and laverbread freshly harvested from the sea.

'Is that another German bomber I can hear?' said Owen suddenly.

'Where?' cried Gwyn in alarm.

'Oh no, it's my stomach rumbling,' laughed Owen, punching Gwyn gently on the arm. The two friends began a friendly scuffle before running off down the damaged street.

On the corner of Calvert Street and Cross Street a bomb had blown the front clean off a building. A small crowd gathered opposite to stare at the strange sight of a kettle still steaming on a stove on the second floor.

'Tea up!' shouted Owen, causing a turning of heads.

'One lump of sugar for me!' shouted Gwyn, as they ran off laughing.

Caer Street was fenced off and a bored-looking policeman held his hand up to stop the boys. 'Sorry boys, street closed.'

'What's up?' asked Owen.

'What's down, more like,' answered the policeman. 'There's a bomb crater in the road as big as a building. It will be a while before you can use this street again. Where are you heading for?'

'The *Evening Post* building; we've got my uncle's lunch,' said Gwyn. 'He's our lodger.'

'What's your name, son?' asked the policeman.

'Gwyn Lazenby, sir.'

'And your uncle's name, Gwyn?

'Keith Jenkins.'

'Ah yes, I know him. A very fair reporter,' went on the policeman as if surprised to admit the fact. 'Now you want to turn round and go down St Mary Street.'

'Thank you, sir,' said Gwyn and Owen together.

'Give my regards to Mr Jenkins; say PC Jones is asking after his health.'

Taking the policeman's advice Gwyn and Owen doubled back on themselves and made their way towards St Mary Street. On its corner an old man stood in the road looking up at the damaged nave of St Mary's church. The main roof of the building had collapsed and smoke still smouldered its way through the glassless windows.

'It's come true,' he said out loud to himself.

'What's come true?' asked Owen.

The old man turned around and pointed to the eaves of a building opposite the church. Gwyn saw a small wooden effigy of the devil looking down.

'When an architect lost out on the job of building St Mary's he carved that devil and said one day it would witness the church going up in flames.'

'Superstitious nonsense!' declared Owen. 'Mind you, the little blighter does look a bit like Adolf Hitler!'

Gwyn laughed, but deep down he was troubled. Surely evil wouldn't triumph? But how could God stand by and let his churches be destroyed?

Outside the *Evening Post* building a billboard read:

SWANSEA SPY
AT LARGE

'What do you make of that?' asked Owen, pointing to the words.

'I heard the other night; Uncle Keith was working on the story. He said it's probably just some mistake, some hysterical housewife seeing things, he said.'

'Even so, if there is a spy and they do catch him, they should have a public hanging or shoot him; that's what the Germans are doing in France.'

Gwyn wondered what it would be like to watch someone hang. He knew that in the days when murderers were hanged in public, crowds of people would go to watch, curious as to what death looked like. These days almost everyone had become acquainted with death in one way or another.

Gwyn and Owen left Uncle Keith's lunch at the paper's front desk and made their return trip across town. They stopped on the corner of Hanover Street to go their separate ways. As Owen began to walk off he stopped and turned around.

'I think we should do it tomorrow night.'

'You mean the mission?' asked Gwyn, surprised.

'Yes, the mission.'

'But isn't it too soon?'

'No,' answered Owen. 'We've got our plan, I've got the key to the drawer for the cartridges, we're all set. Why wait? After last night's raid who knows how long we've got anyway?'

Gwyn knew better than to protest. Owen's mind was made up, and that was it.

Chapter 7

The mission begins

Gwyn clutched his haversack and waited nervously next to the large water tank which had been placed on the corner of Burman Street and Walter Road to help fight any fire caused by the raids. As planned, he had told his mother he would be staying the night in Owen's house. He was not pleased with himself for lying but, like someone on the the wireless said, the first casualty of war was truth.

Owen soon arrived at their rendezvous point carrying what looked like his fishing rod.

'What have you brought that for?' asked Gwyn in amazement.

'Have a look,' said Owen triumphantly. 'It seems I've had a bright idea for once.'

Owen untied the ribbon on the fishing rod's canvas cover and drew it back a shade to allow Gwyn to see the shotgun.

'Good thinking, Owe.'

'Thanks. Have you got the rest of the stuff?'

Gwyn held up his haversack and nodded.

'Off we go, then!'

The two made their way down Walter Road, one of Swansea's main thoroughfares. It was lined with large three-storey houses, many containing businesses, and flanked by huge beech trees on either pavement. With the blackout, the street lamps were switched off and each window and door blanketed by heavy-duty material to smother any light that might alert the bombers. Gwyn was thankful for the clear sky which allowed the beginnings of a moon to offer some illumination; he also knew the Germans, if they were on their way that night, would feel the same way.

Gwyn and Owen stepped off the pavement to cross the road when a growing clanking sound warned of an impending tram. Not wanting to join the rising number of pedestrians who had been knocked over since the blackout, the boys held their ground while the near-invisible tram rattled and thundered past.

'That was a close one,' said Owen.

Gwyn agreed, adding, 'My mother swears those trams are being driven by German infiltrators.'

The trees and telegraph poles loomed out of the darkness like tall, silent phantoms; their lower regions were painted white in an effort to prevent people from walking into them. Every now and then the boys would see the faint glimmer of a taped-up torch coming towards them as people made their way home from work. At such times they carefully ducked behind a tree until the light had passed. Gwyn imagined the warm parlours that awaited those pedestrians and tried to put aside thoughts of the cold, dangerous night that lay ahead.

'Perhaps we should switch the torch on,' suggested Gwyn after the latest people, two women and a small child, had disappeared into the darkness.

'Not until we really need it,' answered Owen. 'We don't want to draw any attention to ourselves.'

After negotiating several more streets (the only excitement being a crater in the pavement, which would have seen Gwyn tumble in headfirst had Owen not pulled him back) they arrived on Alexandra Road.

'Look sharp, the police station should be coming up soon,' Owen warned. The last thing the boys wanted was to bump into a policeman, but the building had to be passed; to avoid it would add extra distance to the journey. Now, as they quietly approached the sandbag-lined building, Gwyn wished they had made the detour after all.

'What have we got here?'

Gwyn's heart almost stopped as a torch was shone in their faces, then quickly switched off again. He could just about make out the outline of two policemen who had chosen that very minute to set off on their rounds.

'Just on our way home from fishing,' said Owen bravely holding up the fishing rod case in his hands.

'You've left it a bit late,' said the officer crossly. 'The town centre is no place for young boys after dark.'

'Sorry, we lost track of time,' chipped in Gwyn

'What are your names and where do you live?' asked the same voice.

'It's OK, Mal,' said the other. 'I know these boys.'

Gwyn recognised the voice as belonging to PC Jones, the policeman who had been guarding the closed-off street a few days back; the one who had claimed to know Uncle Keith.

'It's Gwyn, isn't it?'

'Yes, sir,' answered Gwyn, trying to act as normally as possible, although his stomach was flapping in a rising panic.

'Do you live far from here?'

'No, sir.' Gwyn contented himself he was telling the truth, even though they were heading off in the wrong direction for home.

'Right, run along quickly; and don't let me catch you out this late again or I'll have words with that uncle of yours.'

'Yes, sir, sorry,' said Gwyn.

The boys began to walk off when the other policeman called out. 'Hold on a minute.' The boys froze. This is it, thought Gwyn; we're rumbled.

'Did you catch anything?'

Gwyn breathed again.

'No sir, nothing biting,' said Owen.

'Pity, I would have liked some mackerel for supper,' the officer chuckled. 'Maybe next time.'

The policemen then turned and walked off. Owen grabbed Gwyn's arm and hurried him along.

'My heart almost packed in,' whispered Gwyn when they were clear. 'Weren't you scared they would have searched us?'

'*Na*,' said Owen confidently. 'I could bluff my way out of a paper bag.'

'Yeah, but what about a prison cell? They could have locked us up!'

'You worry too much, Gwyn, that's your problem.'

'Well, I have to worry enough for the both of us, don't I?'

They turned left onto the top end of High Street and passed the Palace Theatre. The impressive building had so far managed to avoid the bombs, but others had not been so lucky. At the end of High Street they turned right down Neath Road. The shops and businesses gave way to terraced homes as they left the town centre. These houses were not as grand as those on Gwyn's Hanover Street. Behind the buildings the boys could just about make out the tall masts and funnels of ships slowly receding into the silvery shadows as the North Dock came to an end. They were now free to find their way to the Tawe.

The streets were more or less deserted by now and any sign of life would surely signal the presence of the Home Guard or an ARP warden; they had to be extra careful from there on if they didn't want to face any more questions that night.

To save time they had decided to risk cutting through the terraced houses rather than following the long road around until it skirted the river.

Soon they came to a gaping hole in the row of houses: a bomb site. The debris spilled out on to the pavement, making them stumble to a halt.

'This is it,' whispered Gwyn.

The boys looked around to see if they were being watched and then quickly began to scramble over the wreckage. Everyday household items lay intertwined with pieces of wood, bricks, plaster and tiles; the house had simply collapsed in on itself.

At one point Owen stepped on a fallen floorboard, sending a heap of bricks and plaster crashing down. The noise seemed to last forever. The boys instinctively lay still and waited.

Gwyn expected a warden to appear any second and shine a torch in his face but no one came.

'Come on, let's get out of here!' hissed Owen.

They frantically scrambled on over the dangerously sharp and unstable debris. On the way Owen grabbed two pieces of wood, each around three feet long. The far wall was still intact, although the back door was half hidden by rubble. There was no way of opening it. 'Quick – the window,' suggested Owen.

Amazingly the glass was still in place. Gwyn went to open it but found that the latch was hidden by a large fallen rafter.

'What do we do now?' asked Gwyn, not fancying crawling back the way they had come.

'Only one thing for it,' answered Owen taking charge of the situation.

Sitting on his bottom Owen lifted his leg and kicked the pane through. A few doors away, a dog began to bark. Owen worked quickly to clear the sharp edges away. 'You first,' he instructed Gwyn.

Gwyn carefully dropped down through the window and looked around. The dog was still barking.

'Here, take these.' Owen passed the wood, the gun and Gwyn's canvas haversack through the window and quickly followed.

The dog had caught the boys' scent and began to increase its barking. 'Quiet, Jack!' a voice called out. 'What's the matter with you?' Gwyn and Owen raced down the long garden and flung themselves over a fence and dived into some bushes on a piece of scrub land. The barking continued until they heard a yelp and the dog fell silent. Then a back door slammed shut. They waited a few minutes to make sure they were in the clear and then crawled through the bushes. Once free of the undergrowth they stepped out onto an open piece of ground and started walking briskly.

Then Gwyn tripped over something long and hard and fell to the ground. He put his hands out and was met by crunching chippings and a cold, solid object which felt as thought it was made of iron or steel. Suddenly a strange sound reached out of the night, freezing them to the spot. Instinctively they looked up to see a large dark mass heading towards them.

'Move! It's a train,' yelled Owen, dragging Gwyn to his feet. They had found themselves on the main railway line; the garden had backed onto it. Taking flight, Gwyn and Owen rushed forwards. The noise grew louder and they just had enough time to clear another set of tracks, and reach the safety of more bushes, before a large engine thundered past. Clouds of steam brushed their faces and they could see sparks of fire jumping around the footplate. Then around a dozen blacked-out carriages slipped by heading for High Street station.

'Sorry, I forgot the London train was due about now,' said Gwyn.

'Not to worry, it all adds to the adventure.'

'That's what I'm afraid of,' replied Gwyn. 'I've already had enough adventure for one lifetime.'

'Well, get used to it. We've only just started.'

The Tawe flowed deep and silent below where Gwyn and Owen stood on its sloping bank. It was around a hundred feet wide. About half a mile downstream was the river's main bridge at the entrance to the town's docklands. Upstream, a lot closer, was a second guarded crossing. On the far side lay a road and then the valley rose steeply up to Kilvey Hill, where they planned to carry out their mission.

'Come on, let's get to work,' said Owen after making sure the place was deserted.

Gwyn dropped his haversack to the ground and took out his torch, a ball of string and a couple of empty paraffin cans which he had liberated from his garden shed. Owen set about lashing the pieces of wood together with the string while Gwyn carefully shone the torch, holding it down very low so as to reduce the amount of light it showed. Once the planks were secured, Owen tied a paraffin can to each end.

Next Gwyn watched in silence as Owen removed the canvas case from around the gun and broke it open. Owen then removed two cartridges from his pocket; he would load up there to keep them dry.

'Spit on it,' said Owen suddenly, holding a cartridge up in front of Gwyn.

'What?' asked Gwyn surprised.

'Come on, this is for Jerry, remember. Look.' Owen spat first then offered it up to Gwyn again. This time Gwyn followed suit. Owen then loaded the cartridge into the barrel and the two boys repeated the routine with the second cartridge. The gun was then clicked shut once more and Owen held it up to his shoulder and trained the sights on an imaginary aeroplane in the sky.

'Come and get it, you murdering swine!' The moonlight glinted across the long barrel and sparkled somewhat eerily in Owen's eyes. Again Gwyn wondered if he was doing the right thing, but there was no going back now.

Next the boys took their shoes and socks off, followed by their shirts and jumpers, leaving just their short trousers. Gwyn stuffed the clothes into the haversack and tied it to the makeshift raft. Finally Owen secured the gun on top.

Carrying the raft down the bank they stopped at the water's edge. 'Do you think it will work?' asked Gwyn.

'There's only one way to find out,' answered Owen, stepping into the river. Gwyn followed. The pebbles were slippery and uncomfortable on their bare feet and the water felt numbingly cold. Undeterred, they carried the raft between them, until quite suddenly the depth of the water increased and they plunged down, the water coming up to their shoulders. Fortunately the raft floated remarkably well.

Gwyn took a sharp breath as the cold gripped his chest. Another few steps and their feet left the bottom and they began to swim breaststroke side by side, pushing the raft in front of them. Both boys were fairly good swimmers, having grown up next to the sea.

Luckily their little swim coincided with high tide, and the usually fast-flowing river had slackened off, allowing them to cross almost directly without being carried downstream. Soon the water shallowed again and they were able to touch the bottom once more. Shivering, they climbed out and set the raft down.

'I'm freezing,' said Gwyn, his teeth chattering.

'Let's hope that Jerry comes tonight,' said Owen, 'or else we'll have to do it all again some other night.'

"There's no way on earth I'm going to do all this again," thought Gwyn to himself.

The pair shook as much water off themselves as they could and quickly struggled back into their clothes. Gwyn and Owen then climbed up the river bank and hid the raft and the haversack under a bush before creeping onwards to lie down in the grass beside the road. Thankfully it was deserted.

'Let's go,' said Owen rising to his feet with gun in hand.

The boys ran across the road and disappeared into the undergrowth on the other side.

Still shivering, Gwyn scrambled up the slope after Owen. He guessed the time was coming up to half past eight. Back home his mother would be reading to Molly before tucking her up in bed. Uncle Keith would be sitting at the kitchen table going through his notebooks. Neither of them would imagine in their wildest dreams that at that moment Gwyn was about to climb high above Swansea armed with a shotgun to shoot down a German war plane.

The lower slopes of Kilvey Hill were covered in heather; the few trees that had grown there had been cut down for fuel by desperate home-owners in nearby St Thomas. The going was slow because the ground was uneven beneath the heather, and littered with potholes and boulders. Both Gwyn and Owen had stumbled several times, fortunately without injuring themselves; a twisted ankle would have been disastrous right then. At least the terrain meant the hillside was usually deserted.

Halfway up their climb lay All Saints Church. The lonely building was reached by a mountain track which led up from St Thomas. Once a popular place of worship, it had been neglected over the last couple of years and people seldom made their way up there in wartime. The boys stopped at the stone wall to gather their breath before jumping over into the graveyard.

The grass was long and wild. In the eerie light it resembled a field of swaying mist. Ancient headstones stood out like islands of doom. In the centre of it all stood the silent church, its stained-glass windows deprived of their colour by the shadows. Gwyn felt uncomfortable; he had visited the church before the war for the wedding of a distant cousin; it had been a happy, colourful occasion. Now the place seemed filled with foreboding, a place of darkness rather than light.

'I feel like a grave robber,' whispered Gwyn.

'Well, I plan to rob a grave of a body,' said Owen before adding, 'at least for another fifty years or so.'

'What do you mean? What grave?'

'Mine, of course!' Owen began to laugh and Gwyn quickly joined in, glad to share a joke in the midst of the seriousness.

'Which way now?' asked Owen once they had reached the far side of the graveyard.

'Up there.'

Gwyn pointed to a rocky ridge rising out of the vegetation. It ran across the darkened horizon and skirted around to their right, high above the mouth of the Tawe and the docks.

'Do you want me to carry the gun for a bit?' asked Gwyn.

'No, you're all right. Just concentrate on the climb and not falling.'

Gwyn wasn't disappointed. In fact he didn't really want to touch the gun. He knew that in spite of Owen saying that Gwyn could have first shot, when the time came Owen would want to fire it. Gwyn was content just to be there. So far the adventure was going to plan and that was down to Gwyn's careful organising. That was reward enough for him.

After a ten-minute struggle up a steep gully they reached the foot of a craggy outcrop of sheer rock. The boys followed it around, trying to find the best place to climb up. Eventually they came to a crevice where the rocks formed a natural set of steps.

'This looks tidy enough,' said Owen, who had taken the lead. 'You go first and I'll pass the gun up to you.'

Gwyn climbed the first step with the help of a leg-up from Owen. He then reached down for the gun, touching it at last. It was surprisingly heavy and the metal, even through the fishing rod's canvas cover, was cold to the touch. Gwyn's hands shook slightly in case he dropped it; Owen would never forgive him if he did. Placing the gun safely against the ledge Gwyn reached down again, this time to help Owen up. In this manner they made their way to the top and after one last push the pair collapsed on the summit's bare edge.

Gwyn guessed they were over a thousand feet above Swansea. He could easily make out the long, flat sea, with ripples that reflected in the moonlight. The town, however, seemed ghostly quiet, with none of the streetlights that had lit up the busy built-up area after dark before the war.

'Hey, no time to admire the view,' Owen said, rising up to a stoop. 'Let's scoot around and get closer to the river's mouth.'

As they quietly skirted the hill's shoulder Gwyn kept eyeing the sky to their right. It was gone nine o'clock now, and if previous night raids were anything to go by the German aeroplanes could be expected to come in from the Mumbles end on their bombing runs at any minute.

By now they were directly above a street of houses which led down to the dockland community of St Thomas. In front of them the ground dipped into a grassy gulley that ran down to the back gardens. Gwyn was just about to say that this would make a good place to fire from, as it was sheltered on three sides and looked directly out over the town, when something caught his eye.

Instinctively he grabbed Owen's shoulder and pulled him down into the heather at the same time holding his finger up to his lips.

'What did you do that for? You scared the life out of me,' whispered Owen.

Even in the poor light Owen could see an expression of surprise and fear on his friend's face.

'Look,' said Gwyn raising himself up on his elbows and pointing to a spot halfway down the gulley.

Owen strained to see what Gwyn was pointing at but he could

see nothing out of the ordinary. 'What am I supposed to be …'
Owen didn't finish his sentence because at that very second he
too saw a torch flashing out into the night sky.

'It must be the spy!' whispered Gwyn nervously. 'What should
we do?'

Owen didn't hear the second part of Gwyn's whisper, he had
turned away and was busy removing the shotgun from the fishing
rod case.

Chapter 8

A chase in the dark

Owen broke the shotgun open to make sure the cartridges were loaded securely, then closed it again with a smooth, metallic click. Gwyn watched nervously.

'What are you going to do?' whispered Gwyn.

'This is better than shooting a hundred German planes. If he's the spy we're going to capture him and march him down to the soldiers on the bridge. We'll be real heroes. They may even give us a medal. Just think how jealous the boys in school will be.'

'But are you certain it's a spy?'

'Who the heck else could it be waving a torch across the sky above the docks?' asked Owen, his voice becoming louder with incredulity.

'But it's too dangerous,' said Gwyn, his alarm growing. 'What if he's armed?'

'We'll sneak up on him. Come on, Gwyn, don't back out now.'

Gwyn didn't reply. He was just about to protest again when a familiar droning sound crept along the sky. 'It's a raid; they're coming again,' exclaimed Gwyn, looking westwards, trying to make out the dark, shadowy formations of the Luftwaffe.

'Yes; and it's thanks to that swine down there. Now are you coming or what?'

Owen started making his way into the top of the gulley. Gwyn watched him go and then quickly followed, realising that he could not let his friend take the risk on his own.

The noise of the aeroplanes grew louder as the boys edged slowly down the hillside. Soon the familiar wail of the air raid warning siren sounded. Gwyn thought of his mother and Molly being ushered to their shelter by Uncle Keith; they would be beside themselves with anxiety if they could see him now.

The boys crawled on their stomachs, thankful for the long grass; despite his fear Gwyn felt like a real Commando, just like his father.

Owen stopped yards from the figure and hid behind a heather-clad mound. Gwyn soon joined him. The spy was standing with his back to the boys, still signalling with his torch.

Owen leaned over to whisper in Gwyn's ear. 'I'll point the gun at him and tell him not to move. If he's armed I'll tell him to drop his weapon and you go and pick it up. Okay?'

Gwyn nodded his head.

'Then we'll march him down.'

Gwyn nodded again and could feel himself shaking.

'Ready?' Owen asked.

'Ready,' croaked Gwyn in a hoarse whisper.

'Go.'

A strange rush of adrenalin began thumping through Gwyn's veins, like the pistons on the Swansea train, as he and Owen silently stood up and stepped out from their cover. The spy was standing twenty feet away on open ground. The aeroplanes were seconds away, judging by the sound of their engines. As the boys edged to within ten feet of him Gwyn saw that the spy was dressed in normal civilian clothes, a suit, overcoat and hat. "Well, you didn't expect him to be in full Nazi uniform, did you?" he asked himself.

Owen held up his hand, signalling Gwyn to stop. Gwyn watched Owen raise the gun up to his shoulder and point it at the unknowing figure in front of them.

'Don't move!' screamed out Owen, making Gwyn jump.

Instinctively the man looked around.

'Did you hear what I said?' Owen shouted, 'Drop that torch and put your hands in the air!'

'Put your hands in the air.' Gwyn had heard those words countless times in Westerns at the Carlton cinema, he had used them himself many times when playing with his friends, but this was something else; this time they were being said for real.

The spy looked forwards once more and let his torch fall to the ground.

'Your hands!' shouted Owen, his voice strong and determined.

Still with his back to Gwyn and Owen the spy slowly raised his hands in the air.

'That's better. Now, are you armed?'

The spy shook his head.

'Good.'

Gwyn thought it strange the man hadn't yet spoken; he must understand English to have complied with Owen's instructions.

'Now turn around and don't try anything. I know how to use this gun and I won't think twice about shooting you.'

The man, still holding his hands aloft, slowly turned to face his captors. Gwyn tried to get a closer look at the mysterious figure's face but it was swathed in the shadow of the hillside. Gwyn wondered if the spy could make out their own faces; did he realise he was being held captive by two schoolboys?

The sound of an aeroplane passing directly overhead caused Gwyn to look up. There was a single explosion in the air and the whole hillside became awash with the burning bright light of a parachute flare. Gwyn looked away and blinked several times to clear the blinding glow from his vision. He then looked back at the man standing in front of them and, for the first time that night, saw his face clearly.

The shock of recognition sent his mind reeling.

'Uncle Keith!' Gwyn cried out in disbelief.

Owen lowered his gun, appearing equally shocked.

Uncle Keith stared back at Gwyn with a look that was a mixture of desperation and sadness. Eventually he opened his mouth to say something but the words were cut short by a whistling scream.

The first bomb hit the hillside around 400 feet below where they were standing. Three more explosions quickly ripped up the slope, the last so close it sent them scattering to the ground. Gwyn and Owen ducked their heads away from a rain of earth and stones. When they looked up again they saw Uncle Keith scramble to his feet and make a dash for freedom.

'Stop!' yelled Owen.

By the time Owen had stood up and pointed the gun, the fleeing Uncle Keith had disappeared over the brow of the hill.

'Come on – after him!' yelled Owen.

Still confused, Gwyn climbed to his feet and followed his friend. 'Who would have thought, your Uncle Keith a spy!' Owen shouted out as they gave chase.

Uncle Keith plunged recklessly down the steep slope, hurdling clumps of heather and scrambling over crags of rock, heading for the row of houses below.

'Look, he isn't my real uncle, he is just the lodger,' protested Gwyn, 'I can't believe what I saw myself.'

'Didn't you have any idea at all?' asked Owen, sidestepping a gorse bush.

'What kind of question is that, Owen?' panted back Gwyn struggling to keep up. 'Do you really think we would harbour a Nazi under our roof after all that's happened?'

'I'm sorry,' said Owen, 'I'm not thinking right. It's just such a shock.'

'You don't have to tell me!'

Ahead of them Uncle Keith stumbled headlong down a small drop, rolled in a ball, staggered to his feet and carried on running.

'We're gaining on him!' shouted Owen triumphantly.

Just then, about a mile in front of them, an explosion tore the night sky apart.

'They're bombing the town centre again!' shouted Gwyn in dismay.

Owen paused briefly to stare at the scene. It was true, the bombs had missed the docks and the innocent civilians of Swansea were paying the price once more.

'Someone's going to pay for this!' screamed Owen before rushing onwards with renewed vigour. Gwyn followed, sharing his friend's wild passion for revenge.

They saw Uncle Keith reach one of the gardens belonging to the row of terrace houses. He vaulted its stone wall and sprinted down the long vegetable patch, only to crash through a wall of runner beans. They saw him fall face down in the earth, obviously twisting his knee in the process. As Gwyn and Owen closed in on him he struggled to his feet. As the boys climbed the wall they saw him limping through the back door of the house and a light came on. 'Got him!' declared Owen.

Hardly pausing for breath the boys ran through the open kitchen door and looked around the room. A family's supper lay half-eaten on the table, no doubt abandoned on hearing the air raid siren. Not having seen anything in the garden Gwyn guessed the owners must have headed for the nearest public shelter.

Owen pushed his way past Gwyn and stepped into a hallway. Looking ahead he saw an open front door.

'This way!' he called.

Gwyn quickly joined his friend at the foot of the stairs. Silhouetted against the fierce blitzed sky Uncle Keith was struggling to make his way down the front path towards the gate.

'Here, if it will make you feel any better.'

Gwyn looked at the shotgun being handed to him. He grabbed it without reply and took a few steps forwards.

'Uncle Keith!'

The man let out a sigh, turned and held up a hand towards Gwyn to calm the boy down.

'Put the gun down Gwyn; you don't want to hurt me. I know this must be confusing for you, but ...'

'You're a traitor!' Gwyn screamed.

'Just listen to me, Gwyn …'

An ear-splitting whooshing noise drowned out the tail end of Uncle Keith's sentence and Gwyn felt himself being thrown backwards through the air by the blast.

Chapter 9

Trapped

When Gwyn opened his eyes he felt a pain inside his head and an almost unbearable throbbing hurt in his leg, just below the knee. He reached for the light switch beside his bed but it was not there. Gradually his senses came back and he realised he wasn't in his bedroom at all; there was no comfy mattress beneath him, just a brutally hard floor. He tried to sit up but his head struck something solid and he slumped back down again. He ran his hand down his leg and gasped in agony.

Gwyn tried to make sense of his peculiar surroundings. He slowly reached a hand up and felt a splintery length of wood above his head. The movement caused a shower of dust and small bits of plaster fell on his face, making him blink his eyes several times.

His memory began to come back. Gwyn recalled entering a house with Owen, they were chasing somebody, there was an air raid in progress, he heard a bomb blast … the terrifying reality of his situation swept over him. He had been buried alive.

"Owen!" Gwyn suddenly thought of his friend. Where was he? Surely he had been standing just behind him when the house had collapsed. Frantically Gwyn began calling out his friend's name. 'Owen! Owen! Owen!'

Despite his pain Gwyn began searching his surroundings and cursing the darkness at the same time. By crawling on his stomach and reaching out with his hands he discovered he was trapped next to the stairs in a space similar to a small lean-to. He painfully turned around and felt his way in the other direction.

His hands brushed over heaps of plaster and brick until he felt something which made him jump. It felt like a hand. Grabbing it with both his own hands he felt on up an arm and then found a shoulder and a listless head.

'Owen!' Gwyn cried, again damning the lack of light.

Owen did not answer. Gwyn remembered the Saint John's Ambulance visit to his school and quickly felt his way to Owen's neck and searched for a pulse. A wave of relief washed over him as he picked up a beat; it was faint and sluggish but at least it was a beat. Owen was still alive.

Gwyn carefully felt his way over Owen's head and along his back until he came to a pile of rubble. He did not feel any dampness, which in the dark would have told him that his friend was bleeding, but he did discover that Owen was trapped from the waist down. Gwyn thought about trying to pull his friend free, but he sensed any movement could cause the roof to collapse and bury them completely, and besides, Gwyn scarcely had enough energy to move himself. Instead he turned Owen's head to one side and made sure his airway was clear. Then he tried shouting for help.

After calling out for ten minutes or so his throat burned and he gave up. 'Perhaps the air raid's still going on,' he thought. 'I should rest for a while and try later.' Gwyn had no idea how long they had lain there or what time it was. He closed his eyes and slipped into unconsciousness again.

When Gwyn woke for the second time his mouth was ever so dry and the pain in his leg excruciating, but his head was a little clearer and he knew exactly where he was. On opening his eyes he could just about make out a faint shaft of sunlight filtering down in the far corner of the cavity.

"It's morning," he realised quickly. "Help must be on its way; the rescue teams will start to dig us out any minute now." Then a shuddering thought killed off the wave of optimism. "The house was empty, the family had left for a public shelter somewhere," he sighed. "No one knows we're here."

Just then the faint light seemed to die. Gwyn wondered what this meant, then he knew. The first drip of water hit him between the eyes; it was raining, perhaps a thunder storm. The drips began to gather momentum, working their way through the maze of rubble to fall in a steady flow. Gwyn moved his head to catch some water in his mouth. It tasted gritty but eased his parched tongue. Still the water dripped down. Slowly the floor became saturated as the water appeared to have nowhere to flow to. Gwyn suddenly heard Owen splutter and cough as he came to. Gwyn gently held his friend's face clear of the water.

'It's OK, Owen, I've got you.'

'What's happening? I can't move.' Owen's voice was faint.

'You're trapped under some rubble. The house was bombed. Are you hurting?'

'No,' replied Owen weakly. 'I can't feel anything.'

Gwyn remained silent; he didn't know what to say. He daren't tell Owen there was no help on its way.

'Did you get him?' Owen asked.

'Get who?'

'Your Uncle Keith, that's who. The flaming fifth columnist.' The anger in Owen's voice resulted in a fit of coughing.

They had been chasing Uncle Keith! The memory suddenly came back to Gwyn – Uncle Keith's face being revealed by the parachute flare. It was as difficult to comprehend now as when it had happened. Gwyn felt confused, betrayed and angry; and now, on hearing the words 'your Uncle Keith', a wave of shame and embarrassment went through him.

'Try not to talk, you need to save your strength,' Gwyn said, not wanting to discuss the matter any further.

The boys fell quiet and listened to the sound of running water gurgling its way through the debris above them.

'But if you didn't get him, that means he's still out there,' said Owen finally.

'You don't think he'll try to harm anyone?' asked Gwyn suddenly alarmed at the thought of Uncle Keith, or whoever he really was, returning to his home.

'Well, guiding the Luftwaffe over Swansea isn't exactly a kindness.'

Despite what he had seen, Gwyn was finding it difficult to imagine Uncle Keith harming anyone.

'But I can't see him hurting anyone face to face,' Gwyn said, trying to reassure himself.

'Not unless he was cornered, and at the moment we're the only ones who know about him.'

That was true, Gwyn thought, but then another alarming notion came to him. 'If he got clear of the bomb do you think he thinks we're dead?'

'What are you getting at?' coughed Owen.

'Well, he knows we're the only ones to see him; it would suit him down to the ground if we were dead.'

'You think he may still be out there, waiting to get us?'

'I don't know what to think except for if this water continues to rise he won't have to worry about us collaring him.'

The water seemed to be funnelled in and was already around three inches deep; even with Gwyn holding Owen's head it was obvious they would be in real trouble if the rain didn't stop soon.

'Listen,' said Owen suddenly.

The sound of shifting rubble could be heard somewhere above them.

'Do you think it's him?' asked Gwyn, 'Coming back to finish us off?'

'Who knows?'

'We're like two sitting ducks down here. And I don't mean because of the water.'

The two boys stopped talking and listened for any sounds from the outside world. All was quiet; perhaps the noise was only a random shift, there must be tons of debris above them.

Eventually Owen drifted off into unconsciousness again and Gwyn was alone with his fears.

They had to get out somehow and warn people about Uncle Keith. But how? There was nothing for it but to sit tight and hope. Gwyn closed his eyes and started praying for a miracle; without realising he too drifted back to sleep.

Gwyn was suddenly awoken by a loud rumbling noise. Then part of the imprisoning rubble fell away in front of him. Daylight burst in followed closely by a torrent of water. Gwyn closed his eyes against the bright light and heard a voice call out, 'Over here! I've found them!'

Gwyn opened his eyes again to see the cheerful face of a member of the Home Guard smiling down on him.

'Hello. I bet you're pleased to see us.'

The initial relief at being rescued soon turned to urgency as Gwyn looked up at his rescuers. 'My mother and sister,' he pleaded.

'Are they down there as well?' asked one of the soldiers looking concerned.

'No, they're at home,' returned Gwyn, 'We must warn them, they may be in danger.'

'One thing at a time, son,' said the soldier, not understanding Gwyn's concerns. 'Let's get you and your friend out of there first.'

The hole was made wider and two soldiers climbed down. They sat Gwyn up and one of the men started to examine Owen.

Forgetting about his friend for a minute Gwyn protested, 'But you don't understand! Our lodger's a German spy!'

'Yeah, and my uncle's Charlie Chaplin!'

The soldiers laughed and Gwyn became more agitated. He was about to protest when his rescuer began feeling around his leg to assess the damage. Agony quickly silenced Gwyn. 'Looks like you've taken a knock to the leg, my son. Someone give me a hand to shift him out of here.'

Gwyn could tell by their faces, not to mention the pain as he was lifted out of the collapsed shell of a house and placed on a stretcher, that his leg was worse than they were letting on, but he knew he had to warn somebody about the man he had called 'Uncle Keith'. The soldiers who had dug him out had continued to ignore his pleas for help, thinking that Gwyn had had a bang on the head and he wasn't making sense.

Gwyn desperately looked around as he was carried on a stretcher to a waiting ambulance. The street had been closed off, but a few people were braving the rain to watch the rescue from behind a temporary barricade. Gwyn looked for someone who might know him, but he was in the wrong part of town for friends and neighbours. Then he spotted a familiar face – it was the friendly policeman.

'PC Jones!' Gwyn yelled. The policeman passed a mug of tea he was holding to a colleague and quickly walked across as Gwyn was being loaded into the back of the ambulance.

'Try not to talk, Gwyn, we need to get you to hospital to sort that leg out.'

'But you have to listen to me,' said Gwyn. 'I don't live here, we were following the Swansea spy. No one will listen to me. It was my Uncle Keith; he's the spy!'

The policeman looked at one of the medics who just shrugged his shoulders.

'Now don't worry yourself,' smiled the policeman, 'We can talk about all that after we get you fixed up.'

'You have got to believe me!' shouted Gwyn desperately grabbing the policeman's sleeve and using up more energy than he really had. 'He was flashing a torch on top of Kilvey Hill. We tried to capture him with Owen's shotgun but he got away when the bomb dropped.'

At the mention of the shotgun the policeman's tone became serious. 'Where is this shotgun now?' he asked.

'I don't know. Buried under the rubble somewhere. Please, just go and warn my mother. We live in Hanover Street – Claremont, Hanover Street.'

Gwyn watched the policeman write the address down in his notebook.

'Leave it with me and I'll look into it.' PC Jones still sounded far from convinced. 'But this had better not be a joke, my boy. Now get him to hospital,' he said to the ambulance crew.

Gwyn watched PC Jones walking back to his colleague, before suddenly remembering Owen.

'What about Owen?' he asked, looking at the medic sitting next to him.

The man appeared a little confused before saying, 'We'll send another ambulance for him; now try not to talk, just relax, you've got a nasty injury.'

Gwyn caught sight of his rescuers standing huddled in a semi-circle looking his way, then the doors were closed and the ambulance drove off, its bell ringing urgently.

Gwyn winced in pain with every jolt as the ambulance bounced its way along the blast-damaged roads to Swansea General Hospital in St Helen's Road. He was still in a state of agitation but was unable to make the medic sitting by his side listen to his tale of deception. Finally the ambulance turned into the hospital grounds on a hill to the west of the town and he was carried on a stretcher to a disinfectant-smelling treatment room.

His leg was broken in two places and he had to have an operation to reset it. Afterwards Gwyn was heavily sedated and slept for hours. It was night-time again before he woke up, feeling very groggy, to find himself on a trolley bed being pushed hastily down a long corridor. The familiar dreadful sound of aeroplanes and explosions could be heard from outside and through an open side door he caught a glimpse of a fiercely burning sky in the distance.

'What's happening?' he asked feeling as though he were in a dream.

'We're taking you down to the basement; there's another air raid,' answered one of the nurses pushing his bed.

'This is the third night on the trot!' said another to her colleague. 'At this rate there won't be any of Swansea left.'

Gwyn wanted to ask about his mother, was she safe? Had she come to see him? What about Molly? But he was hastily pushed into a corner of the basement and the nurses hurried off to fetch another patient. Looking around Gwyn saw other people sheltering, on beds or in chairs. He tried to sit up but was unable to. He looked down at his leg to see it encased in plaster up to his hip.

The patients around him appeared to be asleep or unconscious. Gwyn had no choice but to wait out the raid in silence.

Fortunately the hospital survived the heavy bombing.
Gwyn awoke the next day to find himself on a ward with several other patients, all by the look of them, casualties of the blitz; many had horrific burns and broken limbs.

PC Jones was standing at the foot of the bed talking to Gwyn's mother. Molly was sitting next to him looking at a series of wires and pulleys which were attached to Gwyn's leg. 'Does it hurt?' she asked seeing his eyes open.

'Not if you give me a hug,' he replied.

Molly wrapped her little arms around Gwyn's neck and was soon joined by their mother who then launched into a tirade of questions and accusations.

'What did you think you were playing at?'

'I just wanted to do something,' answered Gwyn. Then turning to PC Jones he quickly asked about Uncle Keith.

'Did you find him?'

The policeman began to take his notebook out of his breast pocket and addressed Gwyn's mother, 'Mrs Lazenby, why don't you take your daughter for a walk while I have a chat with Gwyn?'

Gwyn watched them disappear through a set of double swing doors and then turned to PC Jones.

'You caught him, didn't you? Mum and Molly are safe?'

'I don't think you and your family were ever in danger, but I'm afraid he was long gone by the time we got there. We did find this left on the kitchen table, though.'

PC Jones took a letter out of his pocket and handed it across to Gwyn. 'Although it's addressed to you we had to open it, you understand. Your mum said it was his handwriting.'

Gwyn unfolded the letter and began to read:

> *Dear Gwyn,*
> *I am writing this letter to you in the sincerest hope that you are alive and well. You should never have risked yourself by undertaking such a dangerous excursion in the middle of a Blitzkrieg; and I write this as a friend and not the intelligence officer you uncovered.*
>
> *You are no doubt confused to discover someone whom you looked upon as a family friend could turn out to have an entirely different interpretation of this*

90

great struggle for power. That I am a proud German, who supports the vision of his Fatherland, I make no excuse; however, the fact that I had to deceive you and your family gave me no pleasure.

I do not expect you to fully understand my actions, being so young, but I want to explain that you were all very dear to me and I did everything in my power to safeguard you. Did I not do all I could to shelter you from the mighty Luftwaffe? And could I have left you to die in that house? Who do you think it was who summoned the rescue attempt?

My hope is that one day, when our beloved Führer is victorious, you will appreciate our ideology and understand how I only had your interests at heart. Germany does not wish to obliterate your country, we admire the British people and hope that one day we can stand shoulder to shoulder and share in a brave new world order that rewards our superiority.

You were like a son to me and I had dreams that one day you would grow up to play an important rôle in a glorious new chapter for your country. I trust that one day this will still be so.

Please relay my regards to your mother and sister,

Your friend,
Josef Knefler

Gwyn sat still, holding in his hand the undeniable evidence that Uncle Keith was a spy. Gwyn was shocked. Deep down he had hoped it may have all been some terrible mistake. He stared back at PC Jones.

'So it's true then. I didn't imagine it all.'

The policeman gave a sad shake of the head. 'No, you didn't imagine it. It appears he was not who he seemed to be.'

'But how could he be a traitor? He'd lived with us for years. Why didn't we realise?'

'The Germans have been preparing for this war for a very long time; unfortunately they had probably planted lots of secret agents in Britain, long before it all kicked off. Don't be too hard on yourself. He managed to fool everybody; myself included.'

'But where is he now?'

'It's hard to say. We think he has probably set off for Ireland. From there he'll get picked up by a U-boat and taken back home.'

'Home?'

'Somewhere in Germany, I'd imagine.'

Gwyn found it strange to take in the thought of Uncle Keith's home being Germany and not south Wales.

'But he didn't sound German at all. I thought he was from England somewhere.'

'He was probably educated in England – Oxford or Cambridge, perhaps.'

'Yes,' Gwyn said. 'He did tell us he'd been to university in Oxford.'

PC Jones gave a cough to clear his throat, and opened his notebook, which he had been gripping in his large hands. 'Now, Gwyn, I need you to tell me everything that happened that night. You're not in too much trouble but there has to be an investigation, and you owe it to Owen's family to tell the truth.'

There was something alarming in the way the policeman had

said, 'You owe it to Owen's family' that made Gwyn go cold. He had been so pleased to see his mother and sister that he had forgotten to ask about his friend.

'Owen!' he suddenly exclaimed, looking around the ward expecting to see him sitting up in one of the beds with a grin on his face. 'Where is he? They said they were sending another ambulance for him.'

PC Jones lowered his notebook and his forehead furrowed.

'You haven't been told?'

'Been told what?'

Gwyn could sense the answer but prayed that it was not true.

'I'm afraid Owen didn't make it,' the policeman said, as softly as he could.

Chapter 10

Llandeilo
May 1943

Gwyn watched the pebble skip across the lazy water and pass through the stone arch of the old bridge. 'Now you try,' he said passing Molly a suitable stone from the river bank. The little girl threw the flat pebble into the river with a sinking plop.

'You need to flick it around with your wrist,' said Gwyn looking at the expanding circles of ripples in the water.

'This is silly. Let's go back to Mummy,' cried Molly, turning to run across the large green field towards a ramshackle farmhouse. Gwyn, walking with a pronounced limp, followed his sister.

Although the doctors had been fairly pleased with Gwyn's recovery they had warned that the operation had left him with a crooked leg that would never fully correct itself. It would be a constant reminder of that fateful night. Gwyn accepted the fact, and even felt it a deserving punishment. It was the least of his worries. The loss of his friend was a different matter altogether.

PC Jones had told Gwyn that Owen had died of internal bleeding, caused by his crushing injuries. Soon after, Gwyn had begun suffering horrendous nightmares. In the most vivid and recurring one he was standing in a strange, empty house. There was a loud whooshing noise and the walls began to collapse in slow motion. Gwyn tried to run but his legs wouldn't move. Uncle Keith stood in front of him. The man didn't say a word or offer help, he just looked on in a sinister silence.

Now, over a year later, Gwyn still struggled to come to terms with all that had happened.

After the news of Uncle Keith's deception broke, Gwyn's mother refused to remain in Hanover Street. Despite repeated assurances from the police that the man would never return, she did not want to live there any longer. Although she never spoke about it, Gwyn also knew his mother worried about what the neighbours were thinking. She saw suspicion and accusation in every stare. Although the police had made it very clear that Gwyn and his family were completely innocent, there remained a lingering feeling of guilt that they had harboured a spy.

'I wouldn't take it to heart,' PC Jones had said. 'He fooled everyone, even the *South Wales Evening Post*! Just think, the whole of Swansea read his words and thought him one of us. He was extremely clever.'

Gwyn's mother was also unable to stomach any more of the air raids. She had almost lost both of her children to them and just wanted to get out of Swansea.

PC Jones, who had become a real friend to the family, had found a room for them on a farm on the banks of the Tywi near the market town of Llandeilo. The farmer, Evan Davies, lived alone. His wife had died long before the war and his two sons were away fighting. The arrangement suited both parties. In return for accommodation Mrs Lazenby kept house for the farmer, and when Gwyn was well enough to leave hospital he earned his keep by helping out on the farm. He, too, was glad to escape Swansea. He couldn't have faced going back to his old school when it started up again after the bombing, and explaining to everyone what had happened. That night was supposed to exact revenge, but it only served to deepen the gloom and further destroy Gwyn's world.

Molly, on the other hand, had taken the move in her stride and happily settled into life in the countryside. Gwyn marvelled at her ability to remain unaffected by all that had happened.

'She's only a little girl,' his mother had said. 'She doesn't know any different.'

'Does she remember Dad?' Gwyn had asked.

'Of course she does. You just wait and see her jump into his arms when he returns.'

It had been nearly three years since Gwyn had waved goodbye to his father as he went off to fight. Now, Gwyn watched out for the postman every day in the hope that some news would come, but his expectation was always met with disappointment. The boy had taken over from Uncle Keith in helping his mother write letters to the War Department, but the reply was always the same: 'No news'. Mrs Lazenby would say bravely, 'No news is good news', but he never saw anything good in the empty feeling of not knowing.

Gwyn soon learnt not to discuss his father with his mother. He hated seeing her smile disappear.

When Gwyn returned from the small school in nearby Ffairfach one afternoon he was surprised to see a stranger helping Mr Davies plough the big field. The man was wearing a jacket with circular piece of cloth sewn on the back and another circle attached just below the knee on his trousers. As Gwyn stood watching from the farmyard he heard the clank of milk churns and turned to see the man from the Milk Board returning the empties.

'I see Mr Davies has got him hard at work,' he said to Gwyn. 'If you ask me hard labour is too good for them.'

'Too good for who? Who are you talking about?' asked Gwyn, confused.

'German prisoners,' replied the man pointing to the field. 'They're being farmed out from the camp in Bridgend.'

Gwyn was taken aback. A German standing on Welsh soil? On this very farm? Anger gripped Gwyn and he felt his hands clenching into fists. He ran across the ploughed field towards where the prisoner was kneeling down to work on lifting a huge boulder out of the earth. 'You murderer!' Gwyn screamed.

The German, a rather small, balding, middle-aged man with round spectacles, looked up in surprise towards the on-rushing Gwyn. Mr Davies reined in the cart horse and watched the scene unfold.

Stopping to pick up a stone from the ground Gwyn hurled it at the prisoner, who tried to turn away from the missile; he was too slow and it struck him on the side of his head. He let out a cry and Gwyn saw blood spurt from a cut on his temple as he stood over him. Gwyn, momentarily stunned by his own violent action, stood for a moment just gazing at the blood, but then his anger kicked in again. 'Take that, you bugger!' yelled Gwyn, tears of anger spilling down his face.

Gwyn was about to kick the German when he was lifted off the ground by the large, strong arms of Mr Davies. '*Paid, bachgen, paid*!'

'What are you doing, hiring Germans?' Gwyn yelled at the farmer. 'They killed my friend.'

'Not this one,' said Mr Davies, gripping Gwyn tightly. 'He's a decent man, if only you took the trouble to find out.'

'They're all the same! There's no good Germans!'

Gwyn stared fiercely at the prisoner, who was now holding a handkerchief to his wound and watching Gwyn with fearful eyes.

'Go to the farmhouse and get yourself cleaned up,' Mr Davies instructed the German. Gwyn struggled to free himself as the man walked past and headed back across the field in a daze, but there was no escape from the old farmer's steely grip. Only when they were alone did Mr Davies release Gwyn, who fell to the ground in a heap of sobbing tears. Gwyn had no idea why he was so emotional. The incident seemed to have pulled the pin out of a hand grenade of years of pent-up anger and frustration; the nights of quivering in air raid shelters, the worrying, the bullets raining down on Molly and himself, his father missing in action, Uncle Keith's betrayal and the loss of Owen – all had suddenly exploded in his face.

'Come on, *bachgen*, let's take a walk by the river,' said Mr Davies in his wise, old soothing voice.

Gwyn, suddenly feeling drained, wiped his eyes and quietly followed the farmer across the farm. They cut across several fields and headed for where the Tywi meandered its way through the fertile floodplain below the hill-hugging houses of the small town. Once there Gwyn sat on the steep cutaway bank and watched the water eddying past. Mr Davies stood beside him and withdrew a pipe from the pocket of his tweed jacket and lit it with a match.

'I've lost a few calves in this water,' Mr Davies said, blowing out a stream of smoke. 'You see where the bank leads down to the water's edge up there?'

Gwyn looked to where the land dipped down into a natural ford and nodded.

'They go in there and try to get to the other side. When she's in flood they fight against the current and tire themselves out; if they went with the flow they would have a chance of reaching that pebbled spur down there.' Gwyn looked downstream where the water became shallow at a bend. 'But they struggle so hard they burn themselves out and end up drowning.'

'Can't you put a fence up?' asked Gwyn, wondering why Mr Davies was telling him all this.

'It's not practical,' answered the farmer, nodding to himself. 'And even if I did spend all that time and money making a fence they would still find their way through somehow. Bad things happen; always have, always will.'

Gwyn felt a certain calming reassurance in the farmer's words and he looked at Mr Davies' wise old face which seemed as craggy and folded as the ridges of the Brecon Beacons in the distance.

'I know you've had it hard, but you need to stop fighting against life or you'll end up going under, *cofia.*' The old farmer looked into Gwyn's eyes to make sure the message was getting across, before continuing, 'Just look at that cowslip over there.'

Gwyn followed the direction pointed out by the stem of the farmer's pipe to see a yellow flower miraculously hugging the sheer far bank about three feet above the water.

'Do you think it spends all its time worrying about being washed away on a flash flood or toppling into the river in a landslide?

Gwyn shook his head.

'No; it's too busy living its life. I'm not saying forget your friend, but life is life and you need to get on with living it.'

Gwyn nodded his head silently.

'And I'll have no more of you taking your anger out on Friedrich. He's been sent here to work and you should let him get on with it. *Ti'n deall*?' said Mr Davies.

Gwyn nodded his head quietly to show he did understand.

'*Nawr te,*' smiled the farmer, 'I've left old Bronwen standing long enough. Come and help me get her back to work.'

Gwyn did his best to avoid Friedrich over the next couple of days. Mr Davies had thankfully decided to let the matter rest and did not tell Gwyn's mother about the incident. Gwyn knew it would have greatly disappointed her and would only add to her own burdens. Gwyn went about his jobs on the farm, mucking out the cowshed and feeding the animals, and then in the evenings he sat by the river and watch the fish rising. He found the solitude soothing. Life in the countryside was far removed from the nervous, unpredictable world of Swansea.

A dark shadow of fear still burdened Gwyn's thoughts, he still had nightmares over Owen's death, and he still worried about his father in every waking moment, but he found some breathing space in his new surroundings. The anger which had been in danger of destroying the bright, sensitive and caring Gwyn was slowly receding.

Gwyn still hated the Germans but he remembered Mr Davies' advice and tried to move forwards.

Gwyn was washing down the yard with a hose and brush when Mr Davies called him over to the farmhouse door. 'Take this to Friedrich, Gwyn bach. He's working in the top field,' said the farmer handing Gwyn a paper package.

Mr Williams saw the look of resentment in Gwyn's face and added, 'Do you want to deprive a working man of his lunch?' Gwyn shook his head. He knew he would have to face the German again sooner or later.

Gwyn found Friedrich pulling up thistles in a field which banked its way up to a wood behind the farm. The trees crested over the fence shading the edge of the field in cool shadow, the sunlight filtered through the leaves to paint warm dappled patterns on the grass. Friedrich was singing a song in German to himself. He was on his knees with his back to Gwyn and did not hear him approach.

'Here,' Gwyn said solemnly, holding out the food.

The German immediately stopped singing and turned around to face Gwyn. There was a look of fear on his face which turned to surprise and puzzlement when he noticed the package.

'It's your lunch. Food!' said Gwyn in a slow, loud voice.

'Thank you,' said the German accepting the package.

Gwyn was about to turn and walk away when Friedrich spoke again. 'I am sorry about your friend. He is in my prayers.'

There was something in the tone of voice that made Gwyn realise he was being genuine. Gwyn looked at Friedrich's face. His eyes were kind and his mouth was held in a sad smile; it was not the face of the evil Nazis that came to mind when Gwyn thought of the enemy.

Something else puzzled Gwyn. 'I didn't think Nazis prayed.'

'I'm not a Nazi. I'm a German.'

'They're one and the same,' said Gwyn.

Friedrich took it to be a question and answered, 'Not all Germans hold the beliefs of the Nazi party.'

'Well, why did you join the army, then?'

'People like me do not have a choice in times of war. If I didn't follow my orders I would have been shot.'

Gwyn thought of his father volunteering for the army soon after war was declared. It was true that later men were conscripted, but most Swansea men had wanted to fight. Forgetting for a minute, Gwyn thought about discussing this with his Uncle Keith later on; then he remembered there was no Uncle Keith.

'I can't believe a word you Germans say,' said Gwyn becoming angry again.

'How old was your friend?'

The question wrong-footed Gwyn. 'Twelve, the same as I was.'

'The same age as Nikolaus also.'

'Who's Nikolaus?'

'My son. You remind me of him. Here, I've got a photograph.' Friedrich reached inside his jacket and withdrew his wallet. Gwyn felt irritated and wanted to leave; why was he talking to this German? But before he could walk away Friedrich stood up and held out a photograph.

It looked a few years old and showed a pretty blonde-haired woman sitting on a chair, on one side was a man, who Gwyn guessed must be Friedrich, while on the other stood a boy who did look a little bit like Gwyn. They were dressed in Sunday best and all smiled at the camera, a happy family.

'Where are they now?' asked Gwyn.

'They are no longer.'

'No longer?'

'They are dead.'

Gwyn's anger suddenly died and he saw tears forming in Friedrich's eyes.

'What happened?'

'They disappeared beneath the bombs.'

'Disappeared?' asked Gwyn.

'Our home. It was flattened by a British bomb.'

'I didn't know that,' said Gwyn, becoming ever more sorry for the way he had acted towards Friedrich.

'So there you are. I have no joy in me for war, any war,' continued the German. 'I was a schoolteacher before I was forced away and made to join up. I worked on an administration team. I've never shot at anyone; I just fired a typewriter.'

Chapter 11

The Return

Gwyn bought a day return ticket. He stood on the platform of Llandeilo's small station and waited for the Swansea train to arrive. He had not been back in over a year but there was something he needed to do which could not be put off any longer.

As the train approached High Street station in a cloud of steam Gwyn looked out the window towards Kilvey Hill. He saw the ruins of the row of terraced houses, and could just about make out the empty space, like a gap in a row of teeth, where his life had changed so drastically; he knew he would never forget that tragic scene.

The walk across town brought back so many memories. Familiar landmarks were now forever vanished, transformed into piles of rubble. What had become known as 'the Three Nights' Blitz' had mutilated his beloved Swansea, but the town still breathed with the hustle and bustle of everyday life.

It had been many months since the last air raid. Smiling faces and singsong chatter greeted him on every street. Gwyn stopped outside the ruins of St Mary's church and watched a team of volunteers busily working on reclaiming the building. Amongst the battered grounds he noticed a burst of yellow: daffodils in all their defiant glory. Gwyn looked across to the wooden effigy of the devil and realised that once again, good would resurrect itself.

It took all the courage Gwyn could find to knock on Owen's front door. He had been unable to attend his friend's funeral, being stuck in hospital recuperating, and despite knowing he should visit, time had quietly slipped by. When there was no reply to his knock part of him thought about leaving, he had tried to do his duty, but he made himself go around the back.

Gwyn saw Owen's mother sitting in the garden on the bench he had often shared with his friend. On her lap was Snowy, now white again. Gwyn had gone over what he was going to say a hundred times during the train journey: 'I'm so sorry, Mrs Morgan', 'We never meant it to happen', 'I did all I could to save him', 'We never saw the bomb coming.' But now he was there, he could not find any words. He just stood still, covered in guilt.

Mrs Morgan sensed a visitor and looked up at Gwyn. A cloud of surprised recognition covered her face and then she gave a warm smile. Putting the cat down she stood up and walked over to the motionless Gwyn. She wrapped her arms around him and he buried his sobbing face against her.

'There, there, Gwyn *bach*, there's no need for tears.'

Gwyn's old home on Hanover Street was now the lodgings of several army officers. Gwyn found it odd seeing strangers at home in what, until fairly recently, had been his world.

'Hey up, who have we got here, then?' asked a chirpy man wearing the uniform of a lieutenant.

'Sorry to bother you, sir, but I've come to see if there's any post for the Lazenbys,' said Gwyn.

'And who may you be?' he asked.

'I'm Gwyn Lazenby. I used to live here.'

'I beg your pardon, come in, there's a good chap.'

Gwyn followed the officer through the hallway and into the kitchen. 'Have a seat, young man. Now where are those letters? There's not many this month, they are usually forwarded on.'

'I know, thanks,' said Gwyn, 'but I was passing and thought I'd save you the trouble.'

Gwyn looked around the messy kitchen, the dish-filled sink

and cluttered table top; his mother's heart would break if she were to see her once proud home such a tip.

'Here we are,' said the officer handing Gwyn a bundle of letters from a drawer in the dresser. 'Oh, and this came as well. It's odd, no stamp, no postmark, must have been delivered by hand. Probably wanted to save the postage.'

Gwyn looked at the letter, which was addressed to himself, instantly recognising the handwriting.

'What's up? Look's like you've seen a ghost,' laughed the officer.

Gwyn thought about telling the officer the letter was sent by a German spy but decided to wait and read it first. He knew just the place to go.

Once on top of the steep Townhill slope Gwyn sat on his favourite bench. He looked down at the stone wall below and remembered, with a sad smile, the time he and Owen had tobogganed down the grass on the table.

Gwyn turned his attention to the letter. With trembling fingers he tore it open, not bothering to take his usual care to preserve the envelope.

As he had suspected it was from the man who had pretended to be Uncle Keith. The odd thing about the letter was it was dated a few months earlier. Remembering that it did not have a stamp Gwyn guessed it had taken some time to deliver, being passed through a network of despicable spies and traitors, Gwyn thought. He vowed to tell PC Jones straight after reading it.

Dear Gwyn,

As a final act of my true affection for you and your family I send good news of your father. My sources reliably inform me that your father was captured in

Crete and was taken from there to Italy where he is being held prisoner of war. You understand I cannot reveal the exact location. Do not despair, our Italian allies are quite tolerant hosts, and as long as your father keeps his head down then he will be well looked after.

Yours,
Josef Knefler

Gwyn read the letter again and then let it fall on to his lap. A wave of relief and hope washed over him. It was so long since he had felt such elation that he just sat still on the bench desperately trying to gather his thoughts.

If this was true, then his father was alive at the time the letter was written. He looked at the date on the letter again. Five months ago. Yes, sure, Gwyn had heard stories about prisoners of war being mistreated at the hands of their captors, but this seemed to be good news. At least his father hadn't been killed in battle. The war couldn't go on for ever, and one day his father would be released and free to come home. Surely Uncle Keith wouldn't be so cruel as to play a trick on him?

Gwyn looked out over the bay. To his left the welcoming arms of the pier heads swept out from the docks and the rays of a late sun danced on the reflecting waters of the channel, beating a path far out to sea. The sky above glowed crimson, hinting at the promise of a sunny tomorrow.

Glossary

(An explanation of some of the terms used in this book)

CHAPTER 1: OUT OF THE BLUE: FEBRUARY 1941

Pembrey airfield: Built to the west of Swansea, near Llanelli, this airfield was used by Fighter Command as a base for fighter squadrons during the Battle of Britain, when the RAF defeated their German counterparts in the skies above southern Britain. At the time of the story it was the nearest airfield to Swansea. RAF Fairwood Common, on the Gower Peninsula's Fairwood Common, did not open until June 1941.

Spitfire: Probably everyone's favourite RAF fighter aircraft – if you ever get a chance to see one fly then you will never forget the purr of its Rolls Royce engine. Its speed and manoeuvrability was the main reason why the RAF was able to teach the Germans a thing or two in the Battle of Britain.

Hurricane: Another fighter aircraft which played a huge role in the Battle of Britain and was a mainstay of the RAF during World War II. Although not as 'loved' as the Spitfire, the good old Hurricane was responsible for 60 per cent of the kills in the Battle of Britain.

Stuka: A two-seater German ground-attack aircraft with distinct gull wings, which meant there was a prominent bend along the span making it look like a flapping bird. The other distinctive feature was its siren, which was set off when it dived in for the kill. Its effect was purely to terrify the enemy. And it worked. Have a search of YouTube and listen for yourself!

Sea defences: Swansea beach looked very different during the war, when large expanses of sand were cluttered with hundreds of iron Xs. They weren't kisses, they were large obstacles designed to slow down any invading Germans.

South Dock: Today this is part of Swansea Marina and is home to yachts and pleasure craft. The only worry about dive-bombing nowadays comes from gulls intent on pinching your chips!

Nazl: The name of a political party. Not all Germans were Nazis but few would go against them. Nazi is the short way of saying *Nationalsozialistische Deutsche Arbeiterpartei* or *The National Socialist German Workers' Party*. The political party had extreme views – to put it mildly – and was led by Adolf Hitler, who went on to plunge the world into the darkness of the Second World War.

Anti-aircraft guns, Ravenhill: Also known as 'ack-ack guns', because of the sound they made when fired. As well as at Ravenhill, they were sited at Mumbles, Sketty, Port Tenant and Jersey Marine. You can see for yourself what they looked like, because a similar gun has been restored and placed on a platform in between the two bridges on the Tawe, as a memorial to all the civilians who lost their lives during the war.

Mumbles railway: Could easily have been called the Swansea railway, depending from which end of the line you favour! It was the world's first passenger railway and took people between the town in the east, along the sweep of Swansea Bay to the fishing town of Mumbles in the west. It remained operational during the war but sadly, facing huge running costs and dwindling passengers, was defeated in 1960 and closed.

Slip Bridge: Built in 1915, the popular landmark allowed people to cross the road and railway line to the beach, which used to be a lot more popular than it is today (though not during the war, of course). It survived the German bombs but not Swansea Council, who had it taken down in 2004 and placed on the bay's promenade – a memorial to madness!

North Africa: It wasn't just Europe that was ravaged by the war. The conflict also took place in most parts of the world. In Africa itself there were fierce battles in Libya, Egypt, Algeria, Tunisia and Morocco.

Air Raid Precaution Wardens: As the name suggests their job was to make sure civilians took the necessary precautions in the event of air raids. They also had the dangerous task of patrolling the streets during air raids, helping rescue people from the rubble after attacks, and providing first aid. They would often face the grim task of recovering bodies.

Gas masks: It was well-known that the Germans possessed huge stocks of lethal gas, which had been used in the First World War to devastating effect. In the Second World War there was a real fear that they would use it on civilians. By 1940 the government had issued 38 million gas masks. Most were kept in cardboard boxes with string used to sling them over the shoulder. People were instructed to carry them everywhere they went. Fortunately they were never really needed and many children found they made great 'goal posts'!

CHAPTER 2: THE ANDERSON SHELTER

Rations: With Britain being an island, and attacks by German U-boats (*Unterseeboot* = under-sea boat, or submarine), making shipping to our shores hazardous, essentials such as clothes and food became scarce. In order to make sure there was enough to go around rationing was introduced in 1940.

To begin with bacon, meat, jam, biscuits, breakfast cereals, milk, cheese, butter, lard, eggs, sugar, tea, marmalade and canned fruit were all rationed. As the war progressed, most foods came to be rationed, as were non-food items such as clothing, soap, petrol and paper.

A week's rations for one person included 3 pints of milk, 8 ounces of bacon, ham, butter and cheese, 12 ounces of margarine, 3 ounces of lard, 4 ounces of tea, 16 ounces of sugar, 1 egg (or 1 packet of egg powder), meat costing not more than 1 shilling and 2 pence, and 16 ounces of sweets.

As you can imagine there weren't too many overweight people around at the time – unless you were rich, of course! If you had money you could usually buy extra goods and food on the 'black market'.

Winston Churchill (1874–1965): Many people believe we would not have won the war if it had not been for the inspirational wartime Prime Minister, Winston Churchill. He is best remembered for his truly uplifting speeches which were broadcast, by wireless (radio), to the nation, and gave hope and courage at a time when the future looked very dim indeed. Go online (or look in a *Dictionary of Quotations*) and search for some of his best-remembered quotations – many have become part of our everyday language.

Vera Lynn (1917–): The Cheryl Cole of her times (but a far better singer!). One of Britain's top entertainers, she also made films. Vera became known as the Forces' Sweetheart. Her songs, which included *We'll Meet Again* and *White Cliffs of Dover*, really kept people's spirits up.

Gracie Fields (1898–1979): Another music hall star who did so much to lift the mood of the nation. She spent a lot of time entertaining the troops with songs such as *Wish Me Luck As You Wave Me Goodbye*.

Home Front: The Second World War (like the First) affected the lives of those fighting abroad on the front lines, but also the lives of those left behind. The struggle to carry on and help the war effort back in Britain became known as the Home Front.

South Wales Evening Post: Founded in 1893 as the *South Wales Daily Post*, the paper changed its name in 1932. Dylan Thomas began his working life on the paper but got bored and left after just over a year. Another Thomas, me, the author of *Swansea Spy*, is a reporter at the time of publication!

Medical: Not everyone was allowed to join-up as you had to be 'fighting fit' before going off to fight the enemy. Each potential recruit had to undergo a strict medical (physical examination by a doctor), and conditions such as asthma could excuse you active service. Some, unwilling to fight, even tried to fake ill-health to get out of it, but others objected officially to going to war if they had very good political or religious reasons.

Welsh: Although English was the main language spoken in Swansea at the time (it still is) there was a lot of Welsh spoken in the surrounding areas. Sometimes Welsh words would find their way into everyday conversation.

Bach: Nothing to do with the German composer! *Bach* is a Welsh word for 'small', and is used as a term of affection.

Jam in your tea: With sugar rationed, people with a sweet tooth tried all sorts of ways to get their fix!

Bethesda's Basement: Not all air raid shelters were specifically built for the job. Great use was made of basements and cellars, including some crypts in churches – it wasn't scarier than being out amongst the bombs!

Under the stairs: If you didn't have access to an air raid shelter, under the stairs was generally considered the safest place inside a house to take cover – not much help if you lived in a bungalow!

Luftwaffe: The German air force.

Anderson Shelters: Thousands of these kits for making shelters were handed out in Swansea at the start of the war. However, as there were no air raids in the first few months many householders thought it was an idle threat and had failed to build them. It was also an exhausting job that required a lot of digging, which may have put some people off, but I'm sure they soon found the energy when the attacks did come. The shelters were named after Sir John Anderson, who had been in charge of preparing air raid precautions at the start of the Second World War.

Cawl: A type of thick Welsh soup, usually made with carrots, potatoes, leeks and beef or lamb, but meat was rationed during the war, so often it was like a lucky dip to see if you got any on your spoon or not!

British Empire: In the past we had been far from perfect when it came to taking over other countries and at one time the British monarch ruled nearly one fifth of the world's land and more than a quarter of its people. By the time of the Second World War, however, the Empire was in decline, and following the war the remaining countries started receiving their independence.

Hitler: Adolf Hitler (1889–1945) was the leader of Nazi Germany. He believed Germans were the master race. He will be remembered as one of the most evil men in history due to many of the practices he put into place, such as murdering over six million Jews. At the end he chose to commit suicide rather than face up to his crimes.

Searchlights: Huge lights were shone into the night sky in attempts to pick out enemy planes to make it easier for the anti-aircraft guns to see them and fire at them.

Barrage balloons: Barrage balloons filled with hydrogen were used to make enemy aircraft fly high to avoid hitting the wire cables which anchored them to the ground. They were winched up and down on depending on weather conditions. The higher the plane flew, the harder it was to hit its target.

CHAPTER 3: RUDELY AWAKENED

Rag doll: Girls have always loved dolls and during the 1930s and 1940s, before modern plastic techniques, they were often hand-made out of spare bits of fabric. This would mean they would get dirty quite quickly but, as Molly showed, they were loved all the same.

Canadians: Many people can remember Canadian, and later American, soldiers being billeted in the beautiful grounds of Singleton Park. Others were taken into people's homes, especially in the build-up to the D-Day invasion.

Candles: Although most houses had electricity, candles, were still used at times to save money, and to prevent large quantities of light being seen because of insufficient blackout curtains.

Blackout curtains: Thick curtains or blankets used to stop any light escaping through the window and alerting enemy bombers. One of the ARP Warden's duties was to check for any chinks of light and warn the inhabitants that they could be alerting German bombers!

Pantry: Refrigerators and freezers were very rare at this time, and perishable food, such as milk, meat and butter, was stored in a small cool room with a stone or tiled floor, often leading off the kitchen, known as a pantry.

Palace Theatre: Swansea had several cinemas, theatres or music halls at this time as television had yet to take off. They remained open during the war to help keep people's spirits up. Built in 1888 the Palace, on the upper end of High Street, survived the blitz unlike many other fine buildings and is still standing – at least at the time of publication, as it's in a sad state of repair!

It's a Long Way to Tipperary: You could say it was the number one pop song of its day! It was recorded by the well-known tenor John McCormack in 1914, and was used in the First World War as a marching song by some regiments going into battle. There are lots of reports of people singing in shelters to keep their spirits up – it isn't as if the Germans would have heard them above the sound of the bombs!

High Explosive (or HE) bomb: One of the Germans' biggest bombs, designed to blow whatever it fell on sky-high.

Incendiary bomb: Also known as firebombs. They contained a substance called white phosphorus, which is highly flammable, and were dropped in clusters and designed to start fires to light up the target area for the heavy bombers that followed. Much of Swansea's town centre was destroyed by such fires.

Outhouse: Like a shed but made of brick and often attached to the main house. Would be used as a washing room or for storage.

Bomb disposal team: Probably the most dangerous and unselfish job any soldier could have had in mainland Britain. As the name suggests their job was to defuse UXBs (unexploded bombs) and make them safe –often they failed and were killed.

CHAPTER 4: A PRECIOUS SOUVENIR

Bought it: 'Bought it' is slang for 'died'. In the worst single incident of those three terrible nights in Swansea, which are now known as the Three Nights' Blitz (19–21 February 1941), forty-six people were killed and forty-four were injured when a stick of six bombs fell on houses in Teilo Crescent, Mayhill.

Souvenirs: Every schoolboy (and quite a few schoolgirls) at this time tried to build up their own collection of war souvenirs such as bullet casings and bits of aeroplanes or bombs. They were greatly valued and could be swapped.

Shrapnel: The pieces thrown out by an exploding bomb or shell.

Sand boy: What Gwyn didn't know is that 'sand boy' is another way of saying 'wild boy'!

Jerry: A nickname given to Germans during the Second World War by soldiers and civilians of the Allied nations. The Germans called the British 'Tommies'.

Chums: Friends or mates.

The retreat from France: The war went badly for the British and our allies during the first year, and the Germans, with their superior tanks, steamrollered their way into most countries on mainland Europe. The British army was pushed back to the Dunkirk region of France and the English Channel, from where it returned home all but beaten. Dark times indeed.

Dogfight: Nothing to do with angry canines, but a fight between two fighter aeroplanes.

German fighter plane opening fire on street: There are eyewitness accounts of German aeroplanes actually firing on people on the streets of Swansea.

Adrenalin: A natural chemical released in the body that makes your heart beat faster and prepares you for action.

Eiderdown: Similar to a quilt that went on top of the bed's blankets to help keep you warm. Duvets had yet to take over the world!

Coal scuttle: A type of bucket used for storing coal next to a fire.

Dripping: Melted fat from roasted meat, left to cool and thicken. As food was scarce it made a tasty snack when spread over a slice of bread, especially with a thin sprinkling of salt.

Rag: A slang term for newspaper. (Not a very nice term if you are a hardworking journalist!)

Sunday best: A person's best set of clothes kept for special occasions and wearing to church or chapel.

Cwtch: A Welsh word meaning a hug, or a cuddle.

Home Guard: Ever seen *Dad's Army* on television? Men who were too old or not fit enough to serve in the regular army joined the Home Guard to help protect their home towns or villages.

BP Llandarcy Oil Refinery: To the east of Swansea. It was a major target for the Germans as the fuel stored there was so important to the British war effort.

CHAPTER 5: DREADFUL NEWS

Blacklead: A special polish used on fire grates and old-fashioned stoves to make them black and shiny.

Mam: Another name for your mother or mum, widely used in Wales.

Rash: In this case not a load of spots but meaning 'reckless'.
Cane: Teachers were still allowed to beat pupils with a slipper or cane (a long, thin stick) – often for just talking in class!

Heirloom: Something that has been passed down for generations through family members, perhaps an antique, or piece of jewellery.

Recce: Short for reconnaissance, which is a mission to obtain information. Now you could have recced that for yourself!

Evacuation: Nearly two million children were taken out of the large towns and cities at the start of the war and sent to live in the countryside where it would be safer. Imagine having to leave your parents behind and go and live with strangers!

Swans: Swansea City Football Club. The team played at the Vetch Field from 1912 until 2005, when the new Liberty Stadium was opened.

Weaver and Co's flour mill: Used to stand next to the Tawe where Sainsbury's is now. It was a huge building, the first in Europe to be made out of reinforced concrete, and was a target for German bombs – but they missed! It was knocked down in 1984 to make room for the supermarket.

Suburbia: Suburbs or the outskirts of a town.

CHAPTER 6: GWYN MAKES UP HIS MIND

Brawd: Welsh for 'brother'.

Mam-gu: Welsh for 'Grandmother' in the south of Wales – in the north she is 'Nain'.

Mun: Another trait of local dialect. It's a noun used to address the person you are speaking to. Taken from 'man' but can be used for girls as well!

Tawe: The Welsh name for Swansea is Abertawe, meaning mouth of the river Tawe. The river helped to make Swansea a successful port and the whole town and docks grew up around the river mouth.

Bombsite: As the name suggests, the place where a bomb had landed. If it happened to fall on a building then there would be piles of rubble and other debris. For years after the war there were gaps and empty spaces between buildings that reminded all of the dark times.

Effigy: The story is indeed true and if you look up as you enter the Quadrant shopping centre opposite St Mary's Church today, you will see the wicked object.

CHAPTER 7: THE MISSION BEGINS

Haversack: A bag made out of canvas that is slung over the shoulder.

Infiltrator: Someone who goes undercover amongst the enemy.

Police station: No longer used as a police station (it is now student flats and an art centre), the buildings survived the blitz… just. Have a look closely at its red brick walls on Orchard Street and you will see signs of shrapnel damage!

Paraffin: A type of fuel used in lamps and camping stoves.

All Saints church: Built in 1859 by copper works owner Pascoe St Leger Grenfell, high on the hillside in Kilvey overlooking his works in the Lower Swansea Valley.

CHAPTER 8: A CHASE IN THE DARK

Beside themselves: Very worried or anxious.

Carlton cinema: Was on Oxford Street but is now home to Waterstone's Book Shop. Parts of the original building, including its impressive facade, still remain. It was quite a street for entertainment as the Empire Theatre stood next door.

Parachute flare: As the name suggests it was a flare attached to a parachute to slow its fall. They were dropped immediately before an attack to light up the target area.

Blitz: A swift intensive military attack, in this case with bombs. Originates from the German word '*Blitzkrieg*' meaning lightning war.

CHAPTER 9: TRAPPED

Listless: No energy, not moving.

Fifth Columnists: The name given to those in Britain who sympathised with or supported the Nazis. It was thought that such people secretly plotted to help the Germans invade. The term was used widely at the start of the war when the fear of invasion was at its height.

Charlie Chaplin: Famous British-born movie star who made it big in Hollywood.

Swansea hospital: Was on St Helen's Road at this time. Morriston hospital was built in 1942 for American soldiers and Singleton hospital came after the war.

Ireland: The Republic of Ireland remained neutral during the Second World War, meaning they did not fight on either side.

Fatherland: A term used by Germans to refer to their country.

Führer: German term for leader, who, from 1933, had been Adolf Hitler.

CHAPTER 10: LLANDEILO: MAY 1943

Prisoner of War camp: There was such a camp at Island Farm near Bridgend.

Ffairfach: Small village on the outskirts of Llandeilo.

Paid, bachgen: Don't, lad.

Cofia: Mind you.

Cowslip: Yellow wild flower that blooms in the spring.

Ti'n deall?: You understand?

Nawr te: Now then.

Acknowledgements

Many thanks to Myrddin ap Dafydd for publishing *Swansea Spy*;
my editor, Jen Llywelyn, for all her advice and support;
Roger Lewis, for the cover illustration;
Swansea University's Creative Writing Department,
particularly Stevie Davies, Nigel Jenkins and Fflur Dafydd,
for helping me develop my writing;
and my family and friends for their encouragement,
not forgetting Mal Pope,
who tipped me off to the urban myth of a real-life Swansea spy.